"I'd like to see the person in charge of the Julia Allman case."

Her voice was smooth as silk. For a crazy instant Walker imagined that voice breathless with passion, her pewter eyes muted by the soft gaze of love. Irritated with himself, he shook off the fantasy and spoke in a businesslike tone. "You're looking at him."

She took a deep breath and spoke with little inflection. "Julia Allman is alive. The man who's holding her is heavily built—not fat, but solid and muscular. His hair is dark brown or black."

"How old would you say he is? Can you describe his features? What color are his eyes?"

"I don't know. I only saw him from the back."

Walker looked up from his notes, alert. "You've actually seen him? Where?"

Her gaze darted to his face and held, as though challenging him. "In a dream."

Dear Reader,

When two people fall in love, the world is suddenly new and exciting, and it's that same excitement we bring to you in Silhouette Intimate Moments. These are stories with scope, with grandeur. These characters lead the lives we all dream of, and everything they do reflects the wonder of being in love.

Longer and more sensuous than most romances, Silhouette Intimate Moments novels take you away from everyday life and let you share the magic of love. Adventure, glamour, drama, even suspense—these are the passwords that let you into a world where love has a power beyond the ordinary, where the best authors in the field today create stories of love and commitment that will stay with you always.

In coming months look for novels by your favorite authors: Maura Seger, Parris Afton Bonds, Elizabeth Lowell and Erin St. Claire, to name just a few. And whenever you buy books, look for all the Silhouette Intimate Moments, love stories *for* today's women *by* today's women.

Leslie J. Wainger
Senior Editor
Silhouette Books

Whispers On The Wind

Jeanne Stephens

Silhouette Intimate Moments

Published by Silhouette Books New York

America's Publisher of Contemporary Romance

SILHOUETTE BOOKS
300 E. 42nd St., New York, N.Y. 10017

Copyright © 1986 by Jeanne Stephens

Distributed by Pocket Books

ISBN: 0-373-07127-2

First Silhouette Books printing January 1986

10 9 8 7 6 5 4 3 2 1

America's Publisher of Contemporary Romance

Printed in the U.S.A.

JEANNE STEPHENS

is an incurable romantic, so being a romance novelist comes naturally. Her own romantic hero is her husband, and his qualities live in each of her fictional heroes. Her heroines are one-man women, like her, who view marriage as the ultimate romantic experience.

Chapter 1

Marty awoke with a sense of foreboding tightening her chest. Her heart beat rapidly as though she'd just escaped something frightful by a hairsbreadth. She sat upright in the early morning gloom, forcing her thoughts outward, lest she remember something she didn't want to remember.

A pearly dawn shrouded the window next to her bed. The wind whined dolefully as though seeking admittance to the bungalow. After a year in the treeless prairie of southwestern Oklahoma, she was so accustomed to the wind that she was made acutely aware only of its absence. When she had first moved to Willow, the constant wind had gotten on her nerves. Now it was the rare, windless days that made her edgy. The unusual silence seemed ominous.

She smoothed tangled blond hair off her forehead and felt on her skin the fine grit that presaged a dust storm. Two of the blinding storms had whipped through Willow in the year she'd lived there, both during the springtime. Storms were more frequent then because the farmers plowed their fields in the spring. This was late October, but dust storms could occur at any time of the year.

She got up, donned a robe, turned up the furnace and hurried through the house locking windows, even though there hadn't been a window or door invented that could keep out the fine, reddish-brown dust. Perhaps, she thought, the storm wouldn't hit until she got to work. At least then she wouldn't have to be out in it.

Marty glanced regretfully at the colorful, well-kept rooms through which she passed; when she came home from work, there would be a thick film of dirt on everything. The four rooms would have to be cleaned from top to bottom, the bed linens stripped and laundered. It was the price one paid for living in this part of the country.

When she stepped on the front porch to pick up her morning paper, the smell of the dust made her nostrils burn. Sneezing, she hurried back inside to dress and make breakfast.

Fifteen minutes later she sat down at her kitchen table, toast and coffee at hand, and unfolded the paper. The headline leaped out at her like a physical blow, *Second Coed Missing*. A nineteen-year-old sophomore at Willow State College had been reported missing by her dormitory roommate at eleven the previous night. No one could be found who had seen her since shortly after noon. The missing girl rarely stayed out past ten-thirty on week nights, the roommate told the police. Nevertheless, she probably wouldn't have reported the girl missing so soon except for the disappearance of another Willow State coed two weeks before. The first young woman's body had been found in a shallow grave south of town near Red River, a week after her disappearance. She had been strangled.

The name beneath the photograph in the top left-hand corner of the front page was Julia Allman. Marty stared at the pretty, smiling face, aware that she had seen the girl before. Dread chilled her as the dream she had not wanted to remember thrust into her consciousness. Image piled on image until she saw the scene again in all its frightening detail.

She saw a large room—a kitchen. A round wood table surrounded by four chairs sat in the center. The linoleum had a red-brick pattern. White cabinets lined two walls. One of the walls had a double-sink at its center with an uncurtained window over it. A range and refrigerator sat side by side on the wall facing the sink. The door next to the refrigerator was closed, so she couldn't tell if it led to another room or outside.

Suddenly the door flew open as a young woman—the same who smiled at Marty from the newspaper—ran into the kitchen. Her eyes darted wildly and her mouth worked as though she were shouting something. Maybe she was calling for help, but Marty wasn't sure because there had been no sound in the dream. The door swung shut behind the girl, but im-

mediately crashed back again as a man lunged after
her. He grabbed her roughly. He was broad-
shouldered, stockily built, his neck thick, his hair very
dark. Then, as if a camera slowly panned the scene,
she saw the cabinets, the window, the sink. She noticed a calendar tacked to the cabinet beside the sink.
It was turned to the month of November.

Marty's hands shook so violently she couldn't hold
the paper. Moaning, she let it slip to the table and
covered her face. It had been months since she'd had
one of those dreams, at least one she remembered
upon awaking. She had even begun to hope she was
losing the "gift" that plagued her all her life.

She didn't want to see things before they happened. It never brought her anything but trouble. It
had turned her into a silent, withdrawn child and made
Danny walk out on her a month before they were to be
married. She thought he knew her well enough by then
that she could bare her soul to him; she hadn't wanted
any secrets between them. But she'd put too much
trust in Danny's open-mindedness. He stared at her as
though he'd never really seen her before. Finally he'd
said, "I can't cope with a wife who's a mental case,
Marty." The words had cut her to the heart, though
Danny wasn't the first person who had thought her
unbalanced. She loved Danny, yet was unable to make
him understand that she wasn't deluded or crazy. She
simply had precognition. There was a surprising
number of people with extrasensory perception in the
world, a fact she'd been unaware of before entering
college. But Danny didn't believe it was possible, and
he wouldn't listen while she tried to convince him.

"You sound like one of those fortune-telling kooks," he'd said.

So instead of settling down and starting a family, she'd gone back to college to complete requirements for a master's degree in counseling. Upon graduation she'd looked for a job in her home state. Although her parents had been dead for several years, returning to Oklahoma represented some semblance of order and security.

Even now, after more than two years, the memory of Danny's desertion could bring a lump of frustration to her throat. Dear Lord, she'd give anything just to be an ordinary person. She had spent most of her life pretending she wasn't different. Long ago she'd given up trying to make people understand because in most cases it was a futile effort. Nobody in Willow even knew she had occasional flashes of precognition. But then she'd never before felt impelled to try to change what she glimpsed of the future.

She took her hands from her eyes and looked again at Julia Allman. There was no doubt. This was the girl in her dream. Marty's heart thudded heavily as she realized that, at this very moment, Julia Allman was at the mercy of that angry man. Without knowing how she knew, Marty was sure he was the same man who murdered the other coed. Where was the house she had seen in the dream? In Willow? She had no feeling about that one way or the other.

This wasn't something she could push away and forget. But the thought of going to the police with this information made her cringe. She could just hear them, "Hey another nut's wandered in off the street.

Somebody get the straitjacket!" But that girl had no more than a month to live if Marty didn't do something.

On the other hand, Julia Allman might die anyway. In which case, Marty would have made herself look like a fool to no purpose. She wanted desperately to believe that going to the police would change nothing. They probably wouldn't listen to her. But could she be absolutely sure? Could she live with herself if she kept quiet and Julia Allman wasn't found in time? Did she really have any choice?

No.

But it was going to be dreadful. And just as she had begun to believe she could eventually be free of what she'd come to think of as her curse.

She took a deep breath. Her hands were now steady enough to hold her cup. She drank the coffee slowly and nibbled at the toast, putting off the inevitable as long as possible. Finally, at eight o'clock, she phoned the clinic.

"Dotty," she said to the receptionist who answered, "I'm going to be late. Would you see if Jerry can take my group session at nine?"

"I'll ask him. If the storm hits before then, probably nobody will show up, anyway."

That was true. It didn't take much to discourage the people in her Thursday-morning group. Most of them were there by order of the court. They resented the fact that it was a condition of their probation or necessary to retaining the custody of their minor children. But Marty thought she was making progress with a couple of the members of the group, and she hated to miss a session. One of them might see it as a lack of concern. Maybe she ought to wait until tomorrow.

It was a tempting thought, but she wasn't sure she'd still have the courage to go to the police tomorrow.

"Thanks, Dotty."

"What's the problem?"

"It's not really a problem, just something I have to do. Tell Jerry I'll owe him one."

"Hope you don't get caught in the storm."

"Yeah, that would just about put a cap on it."

"What's that?"

"Nothing. I'll get there as soon as I can."

Walker tossed the newspaper on his desk and retraced his steps to the station-house common room. Grit scraped beneath his shoes as he crossed the tiled floor. Rising wind rattled the big panes of glass at the front of the building. The storm was probably less than a half hour away.

Nelda Purdy, the day dispatcher, was bent over a crossword puzzle at her desk. Three officers, huddled together, sniggered at one of Detective Hemphill's dirty jokes. They stopped laughing as Walker strode past them. Slinking to their respective desks, the three began shuffling papers and tried to look busy. Chief of Police Jess Stout was out of town and Walker, the assistant chief, was in charge. Ordinarily Walker was pretty easygoing, but his failure to greet anybody upon his arrival had alerted the other officers to his grim mood.

Walker's mood was not improved by the fact that
the coffee urn was as cold as a well-digger's backside.
"Nelda," he roared, "are we out of coffee?"

The dispatcher, who usually made coffee first thing
upon her arrival at seven-thirty, gave him a disap-
proving "Not that I know of."

Walker removed the basket of grounds, muttering
an expletive as he dumped them into the trash. Evidently Nelda was on one of her independence kicks.
She'd make the coffee if he asked her to, but not
without a lot of grumbling and snide remarks like
"Who was your servant this time last year, Walker?"
He didn't feel like dealing with Nelda's sarcasm right
now.

After he filled the urn with water and added new
grounds, he sent Hemphill out to the college to see if
he could turn up any further leads on the Allman girl.
"Don't talk to her roommate," Walker said. "I'll do
that myself later." He wanted to do it before he met
with Julia Allman's parents, who were arriving in town
about noon. He wished he could give them something
to hang their hopes on.

The other two officers left on patrol, and Walker
went back to his office to wait for the coffee to brew.
Feet propped on his desk, he reread the article about
Julia Allman's disappearance. Upon a second reading, he decided the final sentences didn't seem as critical of the Willow Police Department as he originally
had thought. "According to a W.P.D. spokesman, the
police still have no leads in the murder of Willow State
junior, Linda Niles, two weeks ago. The spokesman
refused to speculate as to whether there is a connec-

tion between Julia Allman's disappearance and the Niles case." To be fair, that was pretty close to what he'd said. His frustration over the lack of progress in the case was making him oversensitive.

The telephone next to his right foot jangled. He reached for it with reluctance. Before he'd even had his first cup of coffee, it had started—the accusatory questions about what was being done to find the missing coed, the plain nosiness of people with nothing better to do and the frightened demands for protection from women living alone.

"Toliver Vance is on the line," Nelda said. "He refused to give his name, but I recognized his voice."

Walker sighed mightily. Now the cuckoos were getting in on the act. Toliver was a senile but harmless old man—a former professor of teacher education at the local college. He gave the attendants at Willow Nursing Home the slip about once a month and had to be picked up and taken back by the police. "Okay." He waited until he heard a click, then said with false heartiness, "What's up, Tol?"

"I wanna speak to the chief," Toliver croaked, clearly insulted at being put through to an underling.

"He's out of town for a few days. This is Walker Dietrick, Professor. What can I do for you?"

"Better ask what I can do for you, Walker. It's about those young women missing from the college."

It figured. Walker tried to keep the impatience out of his voice. "We're working on it."

Toliver snorted. "Humph. Paper says you have no leads."

Walker slid his feet to the floor and leaned forward, his elbows on the desk. "Between you and me, we don't tell the media everything." The fact was, the few leads they'd had had come to dead ends, but Toliver Vance needn't know that.

"Glad to hear it." Toliver lowered his voice. "I have something for you, Walker. Are you sure your phone's not bugged?"

Walker rolled his eyes. "I'm sure."

"Well, you can bet there's no bug at this end. I took this place apart before I called you."

Walker felt a wave of sympathy for the poor nurse's aide who would have to put Toliver's room back together. "Good thinking, Professor."

"I want your word that you will not disclose the identity of your source."

"My lips are sealed."

"Good." Toliver lowered his voice even further and mumbled something Walker couldn't make out.

"Hardly yellow?" Walker echoed blankly. "What's that mean?"

"No, no! Harvey Zeller," Toliver hissed.

"Never heard of him."

"He's the janitor out here at the nursing home."

"Well, what about him?"

"He's the one," Toliver whispered. "He's a murderer."

Walker raked a hand through his thick auburn hair. "How do you know?"

"I can see it in his eyes. Just stares right through you. Gives you the willies. He's a mean-spirited no-account, Walker. Why, he's been stealing my pocket change for months."

Walker leaned back and stared at the high, cracked ceiling. "Can you prove it?"

"Oh, no, no...he's too clever to get caught."

"Even if you could, Professor," Walker said, speaking slowly and reasonably, knowing all the time that he was wasting his breath, "it's a big step from stealing pocket change to kidnapping and murdering young women."

"Aren't you going to question him?" Toliver demanded.

"Tell you what. Soon as I can get to it, I'll check him out." Might as well humor the old man. Toliver would probably forget all about this phone call before nightfall, anyway.

"If I were you, Walker, I wouldn't waste any time. You should put a tail on him, follow him to where he's got the young woman—the one he snatched yesterday." Toliver paused, then added ominously, "If he hasn't already finished her off."

Walker tapped his fingers on the desk. "Thank you for your interest. I have to go now, Professor."

"All right. But remember, Walker, I never made this call."

"Right."

Walker hung up. Shaking his head ruefully, he left the office to check the coffee urn. The red light was on. He filled a Styrofoam cup and gazed at the eerie darkness beyond the windows. The wind shrieked like an injured animal, and a cardboard box flew by with the dirt. Walker could taste the grit in his mouth.

The worst of the storm should be over in a few minutes, and then he'd go out to the college and talk to Julia Allman's roommate again. He'd questioned her last night, but maybe she'd recalled something since then that would be of help. He might as well make use of the interim to clear up some of the paperwork on his desk.

As he turned to go back to his office, the front door flew open. Wind and dirt whipped through the station. The young woman who had entered leaned her weight against the door to force it closed.

Then she straightened and removed the scarf that was wound about her head and the lower part of her face. Shaking out a tumble of shoulder-length blond hair, she looked around the room uncertainly.

Walker was sure he had never laid eyes on her before. She was the most arresting woman he'd ever seen, and he would have remembered her. She had the beautifully shaped mouth and the prominent cheekbones, with shadowed hollows beneath, of a high-fashion model. Her darkly fringed eyes were gray and haunted. She wore a blue wool poncho and matching skirt with high-heeled black boots. Walker glanced at Nelda, who shrugged and went back to her crossword puzzle. "May I help you?"

Eyes intense and unwavering, the visitor studied him in silence for a long moment. Still waters, Walker thought.

"I'd like to see the person in charge of the Julia Allman case."

Her voice was full-throated, smooth as silk. For a crazy instant Walker imagined that voice breathless with passion, the haunted look erased from those pewter eyes and replaced by the soft glaze of love. Irritated with himself, he shook off the fantasy and spoke in a businesslike tone. "You're looking at him. For the time being, anyway. The boss is out of town." He extended his hand. "I'm Walker Dietrick, Chief Stout's assistant."

Her hand was small and warm in his, and there was unexpected firmness in her grip. She withdrew her hand and cocked her head, still taking his measure. Finally she said, "I'm Marty Newland. I'm a counselor at Willow Community Mental Health Clinic."

"*Doctor* Newland, is it?"

She saw him eyeing her left hand and smiled. For a moment the haunted look receded. "No. Just plain Miss."

"Hardly plain." The words were out before he knew he was going to say them. Her expression didn't change, and he might have thought she hadn't heard him except for the faint color that tinged her cheeks. He glanced at Nelda, who smirked at him over her shoulder. Resolutely he hauled his mind back from its errant path. "Uh . . . come into my office." He lifted his Styrofoam cup. "Would you like some coffee? It's fresh."

"Thank you."

Walker turned back to the urn. "How do you drink it?"

"Black."

He handed her one of the cups, and she walked ahead of him into the office. He closed the door and cleared a stack of papers off a chair. He waited for her to sit down, then went around his desk and dropped into the creaking swivel chair he had confiscated from the warehouse where the city's cast-offs were stored.

She lifted her cup to drink and Walker noted that her fingers were long and narrow, the tips painted a shell pink. Where had she been hiding? Willow was a small town of fifty thousand people; he had thought he knew every attractive single woman in town on sight.

"Have you worked at the clinic long?"

"A year."

"Do you know Julia Allman?"

She flicked her eyes over his face. "No, I...no." Her gaze wandered to the darkened window where the dirt raced past. Suddenly she set her cup down on his desk and leaned her forehead against her hand. The gesture made her look peculiarly desolate. Apparently she was having difficulty saying what she had come to say.

"Miss Newland. if you're worried about anonymity, don't be. Whatever you tell me will be held in confidence."

She lifted her head. The unhappiness in her eyes stirred his protective instincts. He had a crazy impulse to wrap his arms around her.

She took a deep breath and spoke with little inflection. "Julia Allman is alive. She's being held in a house that has a large kitchen. The cabinets are painted white and the linoleum has a red-brick pattern. The man who's holding her is heavily built—not fat, but solid and muscular. He probably works out regularly... with weights, you know. His hair is dark brown or black."

Walker studied her for several moments. Her eyes were direct and perfectly calm, resigned almost. For all the effect it seemed to have on her, she might have been relaying the weather forecast for the next day. He felt a ripple of apprehension.

"This house," he said cautiously. "Where is it?"

"I can't give you the address."

"But it's in Willow?"

She hesitated, then admitted, "I don't know that, either."

His chair creaked as he shifted his weight. He finished his coffee and tossed the cup into the wastebasket. This was turning into a pretty peculiar conversation. His uneasiness increased. Clearing his throat, he shuffled through the papers on his desk until he found a notepad and pen. He jotted down the sparse physical description she had given him of the man. Perhaps if he proceeded as though what she had said was intelligible to him . . .

"How old would you say the kidnapper is?"

"I'm not sure." Her elegant hands disappeared as she shivered and hugged herself beneath the poncho. "Probably under forty. I can't be more specific than that."

"Can you describe his facial features? Any scars? What color are his eyes?"

"I don't know. I'm sorry. I only saw him from the back."

Walker looked up from the notepad, alert. "You've actually seen this man?"

Again she hesitated. Why was she so reluctant? Walker was beginning to have a strange feeling about Marty Newland.

"I saw him once."

A very big doubt had crept into Walker's mind. "When?"

"Last night."

"Where?"

Her hands reappeared from beneath the poncho. She clasped them together on her knee. Studying them, she said, "In a dream." Her gaze darted to his face and held, as though challenging him. "I know it sounds crazy, but this isn't the first time I've dreamed about something before it happened."

Walker sat back, his fears confirmed. First the professor, now this. Maybe it was the storm that got them going. Marty Newland was a flake. An incredibly lovely dingbat. He couldn't remember when he'd felt so disappointed. "Before what happened?"

"In the kitchen I described, I saw the man grab Julia Allman and start to strangle her. There was a calendar tacked to a cabinet with the month of November showing."

He cleared his throat. "How did you know it was Julia Allman?"

"I didn't—until I saw the morning paper."

Scowling, he turned his head to look out the window, aware that her eyes were on him. The hazy sky was visible again. Most of the dust had passed through Willow, headed west. Now the cleanup would begin. Unfortunately, the mental quirks of human beings couldn't be disposed of as easily as dirt. He turned back to Marty Newland and picked up his pen. He spoke in a tone calculated to soothe. "I appreciate your coming in, Miss Newland. Give me your address and phone number, in case I need to get in touch with you." He wrote as she dictated. It was a bit of pretense meant to humor her, and her expression told him she knew it.

Not waiting for his dismissal, she rose and walked to the door. Her hand on the knob, she turned back and said with total conviction, "You have a month, at the most, to find Julia Allman. Probably less. If you don't, he'll kill her."

He stood in the doorway watching her sleep. A confusion of mental images paralyzed him. He might have been a particularly lifelike statue, so still was he. His broad form filled the basement doorway and prevented the light from the kitchen above to penetrate the dank grayness of the underground room.

His wide, jutting brow was creased with indecision. But his opaque gaze held no emotion as he watched the faint rise and fall of her chest. She was very slender, fragile appearing, especially in sleep. She lay on her side on the cot, her legs drawn up beneath her skirt, the red cardigan sweater clutched to her for warmth. A tangled strand of hair the color of a beaver's pelt lay on her cheek.

Her pale face and the slender fingers that clutched the sweater came into sharper focus as his irises expanded to accommodate the scant light. Something flickered behind his eyes as she stirred and murmured in her sleep.

She had tried to reason with him at first and finally had fallen into stoic silence. There had never been a hint of hysteria in her manner. Not like the other one. Only later, when he left her alone, had she cried. His bedroom was directly over the basement, and he had heard her during the night.

She was afraid of him, and that was an unexpected and confusing development. Yet she had hidden her fear well, as though she were ashamed of it. She couldn't weigh much more than a hundred pounds; from outward appearances, you wouldn't guess she had such self-control. A distant admiration for her stirred in him. Inside, she was strong and he needed that strength as much as he had needed it as a child.

"Rita." His lips formed the name soundlessly.

His mother had lied to him. For seven years he had lived with that lie, and rage over those wasted years boiled inside. Why hadn't he suspected before? His mother had always been a liar—why had he believed her? Believing that Rita was dead, he'd left home at the age of sixteen without telling his mother that he was going. He hadn't been home again. He didn't even know if his mother was still alive, and he didn't care. He tried not to think about his mother at all. When he did, the rage became overpowering.

All that mattered now was that he'd found Rita. He had awakened an hour earlier, panicked, because he feared he had been mistaken again. Seeing her had calmed his doubt. He just had to be patient. She would recognize him in time. After all, she'd only been thirteen when she last saw him.

Until she recognized him, he felt compelled to keep his distance. He didn't want to see that terror in her eyes again.

Slowly, his eyes never leaving the sleeping girl, he crouched down and set the plate containing two pieces of bread and a hard-boiled egg on the floor next to the water jug.

Quietly he stepped back, locked the door, and climbed the stairs.

Chapter 2

You okay?'' Jerry Macomber, the clinic's other full-time psychologist, lounged in the open doorway of Marty's office. Starting guiltily, she looked up to find him scrutinizing her, the bowl of his pipe cradled in his hand.

"Sure.'' With an effort she banished the disbelieving face of Walker Dietrick from her mind and smiled at her colleague. "Just thinking.''

Jerry sauntered to the wastebasket and emptied his pipe by tapping it against the rim. He straightened and regarded her thoughtfully. "About whatever it was that made you late this morning?''

Jerry was shrewdly observant, a quality that was an asset in his profession. But as a friend, he could be disconcerting. Marty shrugged and closed the patient file that she had been trying, with scant success, to concentrate on for the past half hour.

She returned Jerry's gaze. With his dark blue eyes, wavy black hair and deep cleft chin, he could almost be described as pretty. Inevitably, most of his female clients fell in love with him. The problem with Jerry was that he knew women adored him and it sometimes made him a little too confident.

Occasionally Jerry asked Marty to spend time with him away from the clinic. She repeatedly refused. For one thing, she didn't think it wise to date somebody with whom she worked. For another, she simply couldn't imagine herself becoming romantically involved with Jerry. Handsome and charming he was, but for her the chemistry was missing. Maybe part of her had died when Danny walked out. In the past two years, she hadn't met a man who aroused an interest in anything beyond friendship—except for a fleeting few moments that morning.

Walker Dietrick with his lanky height and roughly-chiseled face wasn't movie-star handsome like Jerry, but something had stirred in Marty when he'd turned his astute hazel eyes on her and smiled. That was before she'd told him about the dream and his manner had altered. She had known the moment his interest changed to doubt and the moment doubt became discomfort as he wondered how difficult it was going to be to get rid of her. Illogically, she had felt hurt and betrayed.

Instead of answering Jerry's question, Marty said, "Thanks for subbing for me this morning. I'll return the favor. Just say when."

"In other words, you don't want to talk about why you were late." Jerry laughed. "No problem. Did Dotty tell you nobody showed up for the group but Fern Small? She didn't seem to mind the change in counselors and stayed the whole hour."

What else, Marty thought with a trace of irritation. Fern was a middle-aged divorcée with a rotten self image. She came on to every man she met. She seemed to need constant male attention to feed her low self-esteem. She must have seen Jerry as a gift from heaven. Marty had been so distracted that she hadn't thought about Fern's particular problem in connection with Jerry. She hoped the session hadn't set Fern back.

Marty shook her head. "I'd forgotten about Fern. Was she a problem for you?"

He grinned. "Let's just say I'm glad she's your client and not mine."

"So am I," said Marty. Jerry was a competent psychologist, but Marty felt he worked better with men than with women. Somehow she thought Jerry found it difficult not to picture every attractive woman he saw in his bed. She supposed it was asking too much to expect a man with Jerry's looks not to have a good-sized ego, but to do Jerry credit she'd never known of his getting into a personal relationship with a patient. Still, sensitive female clients were bound to pick up when his imagination took an erotic detour to the bedroom. It could play havoc in a counseling situation.

"About that favor you owe me," Jerry was saying. "Let me take you to dinner this evening, and we'll call it even."

"I prefer to repay favors in kind," Marty said lightly. "How about if I take your Tuesday-night class next week?" She knew that Jerry regretted having agreed to teach a basic psychology course at the college. Out-of-classroom preparation was taking more time than he had anticipated, cutting too deeply into his active social life.

His brows rose in surprise. "Deal," he said quickly before she could change her mind. He eyed Marty with bafflement. "You'll do anything to keep from going out with me, won't you?"

"Of course." She said it with a smile, but they both knew she meant it. Poor Jerry. He didn't know what to make of a woman who didn't throw herself at him. Marty's immunity to his charm mystified him, she thought. She was spoiling his perfect record and it bugged the heck out of him. She assumed he was calculating new approaches and was unprepared for his next remark.

"Look, Marty, I'm not trying to pry. I considered not even telling you this, but if it were the other way around, I'd want to know." He sounded serious.

"What?"

"A cop named Dietrick phoned the clinic before you got in. Dotty and I were the only ones here, so I took the call. He wanted to confirm that you were employed here."

"He—*what?*"

Jerry nodded. "He asked what I thought of your abilities as a psychologist. When I said you were one of the best I'd ever worked with, he hemmed and hawed and finally asked if I would describe you as a responsible, stable individual."

"Oh . . . !"

Jerry held up a hand, as though to deflect a blow. "Those were his words, not mine."

"I can't believe this!"

"I know it's none of my business, but I'm curious as hell. Want to talk about it?"

"No," said Marty flatly. "Do me a favor, Jerry. If Dietrick calls you again, refer him to me. I'll instruct Dotty to do the same."

Jerry sighed, disappointed at not getting his curiosity satisfied. "You're the most self-contained woman I've ever known."

"I just prefer to mind my own business and let other people mind theirs."

Jerry flinched. "Ouch, that hurts." He grinned boyishly. "But I'll get over it. I've got a thick skin. Well—I have an eleven o'clock appointment." Still fondling his empty pipe, he ambled back to his office.

Marty closed her door with more force than necessary. She paced her small office, seething with anger. The very idea of Walker Dietrick checking up on her made her mad enough to kick something! She eyed the wastebasket, recognizing the impulse as classic psychological displacement. What she really wanted to kick was the seat of Walker Dietrick's pants! She controlled the impulse and continued to pace.

She should have known better than to go to the police. This was the thanks she got for trying to help! Apparently Dietrick hadn't even toyed with the notion that she might know what she was talking about. She'd always suspected that cops lacked imagination. To be honest, she'd never numbered any among her close acquaintances. Her assessment of policemen as a group was merely an assumption, a sweeping generalization that she would have pointed out to a patient immediately. The trouble with being trained in psychology, she mused, was that you recognized your own faulty logic as well as your clients'. Still, Walker Dietrick had done nothing to contradict her preconceived opinion of cops.

She thought of Julia Allman, and her anger died as quickly as it had been born. Julia was the one who would really suffer from Dietrick's attitude.

Chief Jess Stout summoned Walker to his office at six o'clock Saturday evening. Having just arrived back in town, Stout hadn't even gone home before coming to the station.

Jess was standing at the window, gazing through the half-open slats in the venetian blinds. He turned abruptly when he heard Walker enter. "I'm aware that you've been on duty for twelve hours, Walker," Stout said, "but this can't wait."

"I know." Walker lowered himself into a chair. "I might as well be here as at home. I can't sleep, anyway,"

"Yeah." Jess nodded in understanding, a gloomy expression on his lined face. "Didn't sleep much myself the last few nights. Hotels, I hate 'em!'' Grimacing, he combed stubby fingers through his thin gray hair. Jess had spent the past three days at a law officers' convention in Oklahoma City, and Walker had kept him updated on the second coed's disappearance by phone. Walker knew Jess would have been back home before now if he hadn't been committed to chair a Friday-evening panel. He knew also that it wasn't the strange bed and rare separation from his wife of thirty-five years that had kept Jess awake as much as the disappearance of Julia Allman.

"This morning, Phillips took some volunteers out to where we found the Niles girl's body," Walker said. "They searched all day but found nothing."

"Maybe that's a good sign," Jess said hopefully.

"Have you had a chance to read the reports?"

Jess sat behind his desk. "Yes. Not much to go on, is there?"

"Nope," Walker admitted.

"What about the girl's boyfriend? You question him yet?"

Walker propped his right foot on his left knee and slid lower in his chair. He ached all over from two nights of tossing and turning. "I talked to him in his apartment this morning."

"Was Julia Allman living with him?"

"No, Grimes shares the apartment with two other male students. Julia's roommate says she hasn't stayed out all night since they've roomed together. That's all last year and this semester to date. The roommate says Julia isn't that serious about Grimes. She dates other men, too. Grimes confirmed that. I got the idea he's a lot more involved than she is. He's obviously torn up over her disappearance.''

Jess gnawed his knuckle absent-mindedly. "Or a good actor," he muttered.

"Anything's possible, but I felt he was sincere."

"What about the other men? The ones she dates besides Grimes?"

"I looked up a few she's gone out with this semester, the only ones whose names the roommate could remember. I guess Julia gets asked out a lot, but except for Grimes she hasn't dated anyone since last spring more than two or three times. None of the men I questioned had seen or talked to her for ten days or so. I got the impression they were shocked and concerned over her disappearance, but not devastated like Grimes. I couldn't find anyone who had dated both Julia Allman and Linda Niles. Linda was a drama student and Julia's in pre-law. The two never had a class together, and they evidently have no friends in common. The roommate said Julia didn't even know Linda. There's just no connection that I can come up with."

"But two young women missing from the same campus within two weeks' time is too coincidental to be ignored."

"Yeah."

"What we have here could be a random killer, a nut."

"That's what I'm afraid of," Walker agreed. In such cases, the motive was often completely obscure to anybody besides the criminal. Unless he left a clue to his identity, tracking him down was extremely difficult.

"We'll put a tail on Grimes," Jess said, "since we don't have anything else to go on. Maybe we'll get lucky."

"Hemphill?"

"Yeah, he's the best we have. Smith and Phillips can spell him. He can start tonight. Maybe it'll make the parents feel better if I can tell them we've got somebody under surveillance. I'm meeting with them in a few minutes."

"I spent two hours with them Thursday," Walker said, "and another hour yesterday. I'd rather take a beating than look into Mrs. Allman's eyes again."

Jess scowled. "Damn, why can't we get a lead?"

"Toliver Vance is convinced it's the janitor at the nursing home. Swears he's been stealing his pocket change. How he made the leap from petty thief to murderer, I couldn't figure out."

Jess snorted. "The professor doesn't know if he's supposed to have a dime or ten dollars in his pocket. I happen to know Harvey Zeller. He lives with his mother on a little farm outside town. He's not real bright, but he's never been in any trouble that I know of."

"I routinely checked it out with the manager of the nursing home. Harvey was trimming shubbery around the home when Julia Allman disappeared. The manager could see him from his office window. He said Harvey was never out of his sight for more than five minutes at a time."

Jess snorted again. "Poor Tol. Must be pretty boring, being in a nursing home. The professor's just trying to make things more interesting. A man shouldn't outlive his usefulness." The chief rubbed his palm over his bristled jaw. "Any more weirdo calls?"

"One. Actually, this one came to talk to me in person. Woman named Marty Newland says she saw Julia Allman and her kidnapper in a dream. According to her, the girl is still alive but destined to die sometime in November if we don't find her." Walker expected another snort from Jess, but instead his boss's eyes narrowed in contemplation.

"They used a psychic in that serial murder case in Kansas City last year. I met one of the officers who worked on it at the convention. He said they would've caught the guy anyway, but the psychic gave them a couple of leads that made it a lot easier. I told him I never had put much stock in that stuff. He said he hadn't either, before that particular case, and even now he wouldn't swear that the psychic was anything more than a lucky guesser. But if it was luck, he said he'd like to have her gambling for him in Vegas." Jess eyed Walker narrowly, thinking. "So...tell me exactly what this Marty Newland said."

"Oh, hell, Jess...."

"Walker, it's not as if we've got anything else."

Walker sighed and repeated what Marty had told him, concluding with, "You can see it wouldn't be much help, even if it were true."

Jess pursed his lips and was silent for a long moment. Finally he asked, "How did she strike you?"

"You mean, could I tell by looking at her that she's—uh, a little off the wall? No, there's nothing odd about her physical appearance. In fact, she's a knockout."

Jess's brows rose drolly. Walker ignored the look. Jess disapproved of Walker's fickleness with women, frequently telling Walker that when the right woman came along, he'd fall like a ton of bricks. Jess's tone always made it plain he wanted to be around to enjoy watching that happen. After thirty-five years, Jess was still in love with his wife and felt sorry for anybody who chose to remain single.

"She's a psychologist at the community mental health clinic," Walker went on. "I checked it out. A fellow who works with her gave her high marks, professionally speaking."

Jess flicked a curious glance over Walker. "What you're saying is she's an intelligent woman."

"Intelligence has little to do with it, Jess."

The chief regarded him for several seconds, then lifted his shoulders apologetically. "I think what you better do, Walker, is look her up again. See what else she can remember about that dream."

"Desperate situations call for desperate actions?"

"That's about it. Come contract time in January, the two of us could be out of a job if we don't make some headway in this case. That possibility doesn't make a whole lot of difference to me, Walker. I can retire anytime on full pension. Rose is after me to do it. The thing that's keeping me awake nights is thinking about that young woman and wondering if she's still alive and what he's doing to her."

Walker understood completely. His night hours were filled with the same worries. But he didn't believe talking to Marty Newland again would be any use. As far as Walker was concerned, there were two kinds of cases. Most of the felonies he investigated were the cut-and-dried variety—murders, real or attempted, and robberies where there were witnesses who identified the criminal. In such cases, Walker's job was to write the reports, follow the legal guidelines, get the witnesses to court, cover all the bases.

The other cases, a small minority, were the kind mystery novelists wrote about. There were no witnesses to identify the criminal, and most likely suspects had alibis. But whereas fictional detectives often solved everything in the last chapter with a flash of genius—usually in a dramatic confrontation with the killer—Walker's experience had been that such cases were solved through slow, methodical routine. Piece by piece, scraps of evidence would eventually add up to a picture complete enough to point to a prime suspect.

Prior to the Niles girl's murder, Walker's record as a criminal investigator had been blemished by only one unsolved murder. And that had eventually been solved when a police department in Texas, through sheer luck, caught the perpetrator of four murders with the same M.O. The killer was a madman; there was no previous connection between him and his victims. There had been nothing to build a case on because the murders were motiveless, unless madness could be called a motive. The Niles-Allman case was shaping up to be the same type. In another situation he might have been willing to listen to a psychic, albeit with tongue firmly in cheek. As Jess had pointed out, they had nothing better to go on. He understood Jess's impulse to grasp at straws, but he had a strong aversion to the idea of contacting Marty Newland. He wasn't even sure he could pin down all the reasons why, nor that he wanted to try.

"I'll do it, Jess, but I don't like it."

"I've never found much to like in a murder investigation."

Walker got reluctantly to his feet. Jess was obviously determined, so there was no point in arguing. "If I can see her, I'll call you later tonight," Walker said, his tone clearly notifying Jess that he didn't expect to be reporting anything useful. "Will you be at home?"

"Should be there about seven-thirty, after I see the Allmans. Thanks for accommodating an old man's whim, Walker."

The curve of Walker's mouth was more a contortion of self-derision than a smile. He didn't feel at all accommodating. What he felt was foolish. And he was sure Marty Newland didn't want to see him anymore than he wanted to see her.

It was seven-thirty before Walker arrived at Marty's neat white bungalow on Ash Street. He'd finished writing a burglary report before leaving the station, then had driven around for a half hour. Trying to unwind from his twelve-hour shift, he told himself. He finally realized his reluctance to see Marty Newland again had more to do with his intense physical attraction to her than anything else. Under the circumstances, he couldn't see spending time with her leading to anything but trouble.

Marty had been cleaning the house all evening. When the doorbell rang, she was getting out of the bathtub. She dried hastily, stepped into scuffs, and zipped up her red-velvet robe as she ran to the door.

Her eyes widened in outrage when she saw Walker Dietrick. The deep-set hazel eyes raked her disheveled hair and the high color in her cheeks, and then he regretfully shook his head.

"Sorry to disturb you," he said as though he meant it. "But I have to talk to you."

"Me?" Marty batted her eyes in exaggerated surprise. "Don't tell me you decided I'm sane enough not to be violent."

The strong planes of his face shifted as he grinned. Oddly it was a grin of admiration. "I wouldn't go that far," he said, his eyes glinting at her. "I don't intend to turn my back on you."

She stared at him stonily. "Shrewd of you, Dietrick. If I were bigger and stronger, you'd be out cold this very minute."

"I thought psychologists dealt with their aggression in a civilized manner."

She planted her hands on her hips. "You think a lot of things without much evidence, don't you? Where do you get off, questioning my colleague about me?"

He had the grace to duck his head. "That was out of line. I'm sorry." Light from the porch lamp caught in his dark red hair, turning it to glistening copper. Her stomach muscles contracted. What was wrong with her? She'd never found redheads particularly sexy before. He lifted his head and his teeth flashed white in another disarming smile.

She was confused by his seeming humility. It must be a ploy calculated to put her off guard, she decided. But what did he want of her?

"May I come in?" he asked.

She didn't move to open the screen. "Why?"

"It's chilly out here."

She didn't react.

"I want to talk to you about your dream."

She gazed at him, still uncertain. But then she remembered Julia Allman's terrified eyes. She opened the screen door. He entered the living room, sweeping an approving glance over the rust, navy and powder-blue sofa and chairs, the waxed shine of the pale oak tables.

He moved with a grace unusual in such a tall man. It gave her a curious pleasure to watch the movement of his lean hips in the khaki trousers. Then her gaze caught on the gun riding in a holster at his side, and she repressed a shudder.

He turned to face her, frowning at the look of distaste that flitted across her face. "Have I come at a bad time?"

She shook her head and felt the comb at the back of her head loosen and her hair fall free. She grabbed the comb and stuffed it into the pocket of her robe. "No. Please sit down."

He took one of the armchairs and she sat on the sofa, facing him. He was watching her closely. "You have beautiful hair,'' he said softly, as though he spoke to himself.

A shiver skipped up Marty's spine and she remembered the animal grace with which he moved. Such strong sexual awareness was out of character for her. She shifted uncomfortably, and decided it would be prudent to let him know right away that she didn't take such bald flattery seriously. She cleared her throat. ''I told you everything I could remember about the dream. Besides, I know you didn't believe me.''

He stirred, pulling his mind back to the business at hand. He took out a pen and a small notepad. ''I didn't say that, Marty.''

It was the first time he'd called her by her first name, and it lent an odd intimacy to the meeting that bothered her. She was suddenly too aware of her nudity beneath the robe. Her first instinct was to argue with him, as much to dispel the sexual tension she felt as to remind him that his manner Thursday morning had spoken louder than his words. But she restrained herself. What mattered was Julia Allman's fate, not Marty's injured pride or her awareness of Walker Dietrick's blatant masculinity.

''Would you mind going through it once more for me?'' he asked.

She wondered what had brought on his about-face. Something told her she was all the police had, and they were desperate enough to consider anything. Well, it didn't matter, as long as they were willing to give her the benefit of the doubt. ''I'll go through it ten times if it'll help you find that girl.'' She repeated what she had told him Thursday almost word for word. "I wish I could tell you more," she concluded.

"How tall did the kidnapper seem to you?"

She shook her head. "It's hard to judge. Wait a minute.... How tall is Julia Allman?"

"Five-feet-four."

Marty closed her eyes in order to recall the dream more clearly. "If she's five-four," she mused, "I think he's about five-nine or ten." She opened her eyes. "Is that any help to you?"

"Every new detail is more than we knew before," he said noncommittally.

"You don't really believe I have precognition, do you?"

He shrugged. "I'm reserving judgement. Would you be willing to come for a drive with me? If we pass the house you saw in your dream, maybe you'll sense something." He felt like a fool seriously suggesting it. He had little hope she could find the house, if it existed at all. What he wanted, he realized, was simply to spend some time with her. If this woman was trouble, he thought, he was ready at that moment to walk right into it.

She sighed. "What you're talking about is clairvoyance, not precognition. Obviously you know nothing about extrasensory perception."

"Maybe you'd better educate me then, if we're going to work together. You could begin over dinner—if you haven't already eaten."

"No," she murmured, "I haven't." What did he mean, work together? He was asking her to tell him about extrasensory perception, yet she sensed that wasn't his real interest in her at all. And she wanted to go with him, to be with him. More troubling still, she sensed that he was equally aware of the electricity between them. His hazel eyes smiled at her. Half mesmerized, she rose and glided across the room. "I'll get dressed."

Chapter 3

I'm still not convinced this isn't a waste of time." Marty had resigned herself; she was doing this for Julia Allman. But she wanted Walker to know she recognized the skepticism lurking in his thick-lashed eyes. They were seated at a table in Emil's Country Inn, a restaurant noted for its delicious Lebanese appetizers. After ordering T-bones, they were taking the edge off their hunger with cabbage rolls and tabbouleh. A candle affixed to the wall enclosed the table in a flickering intimacy.

His grin would have been insolent if not for the candid curiosity edging out the doubt in his eyes. Every time he turned that smile on her, her pulse fluttered.

Whether it was intellectual pride or the effect his raw masculinity was having on her emotions, she wasn't sure. What was clear was that his opinion mattered to her. After two years, she'd grown comfortable with her detachment from men. Now, all of a sudden, she thought she could lose her head over this man if given half a chance.

Amazing—this adolescent giddiness that she hadn't felt in a decade. Walker Dietrick was the last man she should allow to disorder her neatly arranged life. He thought her eccentric at best, at worst, unbalanced. Her attitudes as a behavioral scientist and those she perceived to be necessary for a career in law enforcement were poles apart. Fingering the gold chain about her neck, she tried to judge his age. About thirty, she guessed. He'd been raised in Willow and evidently intended to die there, while her professional goals could never be attained in such an isolated backwater. But none of that was insurmountable. The sticking point was the fact that Danny's desertion was burned in her brain. There was no scar as deep as that inflicted by a betrayal of love. She wasn't about to open herself to that again.

"You have something better to do?"

It was a rhetorical question. She'd already admitted she had no plans for the evening. She dropped the neck chain to smooth the ruffle that outlined the scooped neck of her dress. "It's just that parapsychology isn't a sideshow or a joke. It's a serious matter to me."

As his eyes made an appreciative assessment of her, she was foolishly glad she'd worn a softly feminine dress of rose crepe. "I'm willing to admit my opinion on the subject is hardly educated," he said with little-

boy ingenuousness that threatened to disarm her. The
man was a seeming paradox, and she had always been
intrigued by puzzles. It must be the combination of
youthful charm and the masculine experience glinting
in his eyes that she found so appealing.

She brought her napkin to her lips to hide a smile as
she said, "Ignorant opinions are usually more en-
trenched than educated ones."

He appraised her carefully. "You're determined to
make me pay for Thursday, aren't you?" The waver-
ing candle flame highlighted the rugged planes and
hollows of his face. "I've already apologized."

"Words are cheap."

He shrugged, his eyes sparkling with amusement.
"Considering the way you greeted me earlier this evening, maybe I should be grateful to be getting a
tongue-lashing instead of a whip."

Remembering her childish impulse to kick a wastebasket, she bantered, "Oh, one good swift kick would
suffice."

He flinched and drawled unabashedly, "Where it
would do the most damage, no doubt."

Her playful mood died in the heat of embarrass-
ment. But she would choke before she let him know
his sexual innuendo had literally taken her breath.
Somehow she had to give as good as she got. "The
idea has a certain appeal," she managed.

Teasing laughter lurked in his narrowed eyes. "You
might have a point."

Why had she thought she could engage in repartee
with this man? She concentrated on cutting a piece of
her cabbage roll. "Why on earth would you say that?"

She looked up to find him staring bemusedly at her mouth. "Because I'd have to take preventive action, and I can think of several very enjoyable ones."

Well, she'd gotten herself into this. She'd just have to muddle through. "I can't." She clutched frantically at the old, familiar detachment—her security blanket—and gazed back at him.

He stopped smiling and in a perfectly solemn tone said "I'd be happy to demonstrate."

She was suddenly intensely aware of their physical differences. The hair she wound nervously around her finger was fine and soft; his was thick and coarse, sweeping with springing vigor across his forehead. Her smooth skin looked as pale as bone china in the candlelight, but his was ruddy and hair-roughened. Her slender fingers were fragile in comparison with the strength of his big-boned hands. For the first time in years, she felt totally feminine.

Here she sat with an officer of the law, a guardian of the people, and she felt about as safe as she would with a cornered copperhead! Careful. She must be very careful.

The waiter brought their steaks, giving Marty time to reorder her wayward thoughts. "Well," she said as she split her baked potato and added butter. "I might as well start. You did invite me to dinner to talk about extrasensory perception."

Walker reached for his steak knife with an expression that might have been regret and followed her lead. "So I did." His big hands made the knife and fork he held look like a child's toys. Everything about him gave off an aura of strength, even his long fingers with the square-trimmed nails.

"I read in the newspaper about ESP occasionally," he continued. "Who doesn't? But most people are like me. They throw the term around without fully understanding it."

She had to smile. His admission seemed sincere, his interest in the subject real. She sampled her steak and found it cooked to perfection. "I have a theory about why the term ESP has been so widely appropriated. It fills a need. It gives a label to the puzzling experiences many people have." She watched him take a bite of steak and chew ponderingly. "Doubting Thomases might call the occurrences delusion or imagination, but the people involved know those words don't describe what happened to them."

He grinned. "I get the message."

He was a good sport. She liked that. She ate more of her steak and potato before continuing. "ESP is a blanket term used for any experience where information is secured without the senses—telepathy, clairvoyance, precognition." She paused and smiled self-consciously. "I don't mean to sound like I'm lecturing you."

He waved his fork. "Go ahead."

"Well . . . telepathy means knowing what another person is thinking or feeling. Clairvoyance is the ability to perceive objects or events occurring in the present that can't be perceived through the five senses. Precognition, of course, means knowing something before it happens."

"Like your dream."

She nodded.

He reached for his water glass. He drank slowly, considering her. Setting the glass down, he said, "Look into the future and tell me if you see us spending a lot of time together."

She frowned. "I thought you wanted to hear this."

His auburn brows arched roguishly. "Sorry. But you have such a gorgeous mouth." Her frown deepened and he added hastily, "Okay, I'll get serious." His eyes twinkled. "Not that I'm not serious about your mouth."

"Walker..."

She took a couple of deep breaths to calm the erratic beat of her heart. She'd handled flirts before. Why couldn't she handle this one? She sighed and concentrated on picking up pieces of potato with her fork.

"I really was listening, Marty," he assured her. "Telepathy, clairvoyance, precognition. See? Which category does moving objects with your mind come under?"

"That's another area—psychokinesis or PK. Researchers don't know how PK or ESP work. The process is an unknown. The Greek letter *psi* is the general term used to refer to phenomena in all categories. It's like the x in algebra—noncommittal, an unknown quantity."

"There are serious scientists looking into this?"

"Of course. Ever since the 1930s."

"What you're saying is they can define ESP and break it down into categories, but they can't explain it."

"Yes."

He motioned for the waitress to refill his coffee cup. After swallowing a sip from the filled cup, he said, "I guess what I'd really like to know more about is you. When did you first think you had precognition?"

Carefully she smoothed her paper napkin on her lap and met his level gaze. "I didn't know it was precognition until I was a freshman in college. The way my parents and friends reacted when I told them about it when I was a kid made me wonder if there was something wrong with me. I learned to keep it to myself. In a basic psychology course, I finally discovered there were many other people who had similar experiences. When I heard that, it felt as though the weight of the world rolled off my shoulders."

He was totally serious now, flirtation momentarily forgotten. His expression was very grave. Something in her tone told him that her problems over her ability, or whatever it was, hadn't ended when she was eighteen. "But it hasn't been all smooth sailing since then, has it?"

A sadness passed over her face. "No, far from it. There are too many people like my parents and childhood friends—contemptuous or afraid of things they don't understand."

His lips curved in a lopsided, sympathetic smile. "I'm sorry," he said softly. "Would you tell me about the first precognitive experience you can remember?"

She hadn't expected gentleness from him. In spite of first impressions, he wasn't a simple man. It might take a lifetime to discover all his varying facets. She caught herself up short. What was she thinking? She brought her mind back to his request. It wasn't pleasant for her to recall that part of her childhood. But he seemed to be listening with an open mind, and she had come to dinner knowing what they would talk about. If she could convince him of the genuineness of her precognition, he might take her dream seriously. She had to try; Julia Allman had such a short time to live....

"I was nine years old. I was sitting on my bed, playing with my dolls. There was an old family portrait of my maternal grandfather hanging over the bed. All at once I was hot all over and I felt compelled to turn and look at my grandfather's portrait. At that precise moment, the string from which the picture hung broke and it fell onto my bed, and a dead certainty filled me. I was convinced my grandfather was in trouble. I began to cry and ran to find my mother. I told her Grandfather was hurt. She tried to reassure me, and I became hysterical." Marty smiled wryly. "To humor me, she would have called my grandparents, but they didn't have a phone. So she put me to bed and told me to take a nap and when I woke up I'd feel much better."

"Did you?"

"Fall asleep? Yes. But I didn't feel better when I woke up. I went around feeling depressed for three days and then a telegram came from my grandmother. It said my grandfather had suffered a light heart attack and was in the hospital, but he was much better and was going home in a day or two. Apparently Grandmother hadn't thought it serious enough to find a telephone and call us immediately. My grandmother had a thing about worrying people unnecessarily.''

''And the attack occurred shortly after the picture fell.'' It wasn't a question.

''Right. Three hours to be exact. My parents discussed the 'coincidence' over dinner and, as far as I know, it was never mentioned after that. After a few other 'coincidences,' my mother told me if I didn't stop making up stories, I wouldn't have any friends.'' Marty sighed. ''Her intentions were good. She just didn't know what she was doing.''

''So you became a psychologist.''

She'd been right about the facets. He was more perceptive than she'd imagined. ''Yes. I wanted to know what makes people tick. I wanted to understand myself—and my parents. They did the best they could—but were simply ignorant of child psychology.''

They finished eating. Walker leaned his square chin on a fist. He was a good listener. He might not agree with what he heard, but he paid close attention to what she said. After she finished speaking, he remained silent for a long moment. Finally he asked, ''Where are they now?''

''Dead. Within a year of each other.''

''Any brothers or sisters?''

She shook her head. ''I think that was part of the problem. All their attention and aspirations were centered on me. I suppose that's why my mother couldn't accept the possibility that I was in any way different from the children of her friends. She was inordinately concerned about what people thought. In her mind, my 'overactive imagination,' as she called it, assumed far too much importance." Marty laughed softly. "Mother had an aunt who the family called 'peculiar.' They hid her away in an upstairs bedroom where she slowly went mad. I think Mother was always afraid I'd turn out like her Aunt Bess."

She was surprised to see him grimace, as though her remembered childhood pain hurt him. He threw a bill on the table. "I need some fresh air. Let's go for a drive."

"Next time we go out together, I'll use my own car. I hope you don't feel too conspicuous." They were in Walker's police car, cruising slowly through Willow's "downtown," which contained about six square blocks of businesses. The southwestern corner of Oklahoma being sparsely settled, Willow was the shopping hub for people living on farms and in smaller towns in a fifty-mile radius. Consequently its economic climate was fairly healthy, even though that portion of the state was losing population slowly but steadily. Willow State College, with its fifteen-thousand-plus students, played a large part in the town's continued prosperity. It was a source of amazement to Marty that college students seemed to have so much money to spend.

She glanced sideways at Walker. Judging from his last remark, he took it for granted that they would be going out together again. She wondered if the reason was the Julia Allman case or a more personal one, but she didn't dare ask. After the restaurant, she thought it would be wise not to give Walker any more open-

ings. Nevertheless, she couldn't deny the chaotic effect his touch had had on her when his hand had
settled lightly against the small of her back to guide
her from the restaurant. Right now, a thrill fluttered
through her at the thought of seeing him again. She
simply must get hold of herself and squash this
schoolgirl crush before it got any worse. But it was
difficult, sitting so close to him in the small enclosure
of the front seat.

"This is fine," she said. "I've never ridden in a police car before. I only hope one of my clients doesn't
see me and think I've been arrested."

Walker laughed, a glimpse of white teeth revealed
in the light from the dash. "Don't worry. I'll vouch for
you." Casually he reached for her hand, which lay in
her lap. His big hand completely enveloped hers in
warm intimacy.

"What are you doing?" she said inanely, her composure shattered.

He laughed again. "Relax, Marty. I never try to seduce a woman on the first date."

"I wouldn't call this a date," she protested.

He smiled enigmatically. "Tell me more about
ESP."

She squinted at him suspiciously, wondering if the
change of subject was meant to divert her attention
from the fact that he had not released her hand. She
sighed and relaxed against the seat. It was nothing to
make a federal case out of. Besides, she admitted, she
liked the feel of her hand in his.

"The truth is there aren't many objective facts to tell. Even researchers who've been studying it for years can't always be sure if an experience is true ESP or not. A person may think he's received information without sensory mediation, but the distinction between new information and information derived from past experiences may not be clear."

"I'm not sure I understand what you're saying."

"Well, suppose a woman is pregnant after having several miscarriages, and she becomes convinced she will lose the baby she is carrying, as well. If, in fact, she does miscarry, did she have true precognition? Or was her conviction a psychological defense against another disappointment, in case the pregnancy turned out like the previous ones? There's even a possibility that her mental attitude could cause the miscarriage."

"A self-fulfilling prophecy?"

"Yes, though the process would be unconscious and the opposite of what her conscious self really wanted. I once counseled a woman who was absolutely convinced she would die at the age of fifty-one because both her mother and grandmother had died at that age. Nothing I said made a dent in her conviction."

"Did she die?"

"Yes, from a perforated ulcer, two days before her fifty-second birthday. I can't prove it, but I don't think she had precognition. Because of her mother and grandmother, she became fixated on fifty-one as the age at which she would die. She then, in effect, made it happen. She was an extremely anxious woman with a ten-year history of ulcers. Just before and during her fifty-first year, when I was seeing her, her anxiety increased markedly." Marty sighed again. "Neither I, nor a psychiatrist she worked with during that period of time, could make her see she was her own worst enemy."

"Head games," he murmured. "I see it in my work, too. Every guy I've arrested can explain away his own responsibility for what he's done. It's always somebody else's fault when he ends up in jail."

They rode in silence for a while. Marty was exquisitely aware of the pressure of his hand against her thigh. "Is that what you think my dream was, a head game?"

He had the good grace to flinch sheepishly. "I'm going to be honest with you, Marty. I don't know. Isn't it possible you could have seen Julia Allman somewhere before she appeared in your dream? Willow's not a very big town. You could easily have seen her, and then forgotten it."

She tried to sound as though she didn't care about his opinion of her. "It's possible, yes. But I didn't know she'd been kidnapped until after I had the dream. Can you explain that?"

"No, I can't explain it. That's what makes the whole thing so frustrating. I prefer dealing with what I can understand. The problem is that, in this instance, we just don't have anything to work with."

"So I'm the last resort, only slightly better than nothing." She gazed out the side window. They were driving slowly through residential streets lined with modest homes.

He glanced at her. "Do you want me to try to make you feel better, or be honest?"

She sniffed. "Don't give my feelings a second thought."

"Okay then. Yes, you could say this is a last resort. I'm going to drive around for a while. If you get any feelings about a certain house, just tell me."

"For starters," she sighed, "there are a couple of things wrong with that approach. First, you're asking me to get a clairvoyant impression on command. ESP doesn't operate on command. Furthermore, the fact that I have precognition doesn't mean I'm more clairvoyant than the next person."

"You mean you can have one kind of ESP and not the others?"

"Yes. In my case, at least, most of the experiences I've had have been precognitive. Of course I've never tried anything like this before."

He released her hand and gripped the steering wheel. "Well, try now," he said impatiently. "I'll keep quiet so you can concentrate."

She did try, but she knew almost immediately that it wasn't going to work. From her reading of the research, she knew that in controlled experiments, even good reliable ESP subjects were usually adversely affected if a visitor came into the experimental room. Observers seemed to produce self-consciousness in the subject, which interfered with the state of mind necessary for the information secured by ESP to break through into awareness. She didn't tell Walker any of this, though. It sounded too much like the rationalization he said criminals were adept at.

Marty's personal discomfort was increased by simply being with Walker. She found him far too attractive to be able to relax sufficiently to receive impressions from the subconscious. After a half hour of driving around in virtual silence, she said, "It's just not going to work. I'm sorry."

He expelled a long breath, as though he truly had been hoping for something and was disappointed. "Thanks for trying, anyway. I'll drive you back to your house now."

The night was autumn crisp when they stepped from the car, and the ever-present wind was like the slice of a knife. She was grateful for the warmth of her jacket. She was expecting the weight of his hand on her back this time as he guided her toward the front door.

"Don't feel bad," he said easily. "The evening wasn't a total loss."

They had reached her front porch, and when she turned to face him, he placed his hands lightly on her shoulders. She could make out his face in the moon's light, but his expression gave her no clue as to whether he was teasing or not.

"Thank you for dinner," she murmured.

He chuckled huskily. "Thank you for the charming company."

She thought he was teasing her, but she couldn't be sure. She fumbled in her pocket for her door key. Drawing it out, she turned toward the door.

Before she could fit the key into the lock, he turned her back to face him. "Not so fast, Marty." Then he cupped her face with his big hands. "I've been wanting to kiss you all evening."

"Oh," she gasped, "I don't think—"

Bending his head, he brought his mouth down to hers. His lips were warm and incredibly arousing. When she tried to turn her head, he held it gently but firmly still while he deepened the kiss. "Marty," he whispered into her mouth, "you taste as good as you look."

No longer trying to break the kiss, she leaned against him. His hands moved to mold her shoulders, then slid with slow, caressing strokes, down to her hips.

The hot, moist invitation of his mouth sent excitement surging through her veins with her pounding blood. She felt more alive than she had felt in years. Her lips softened and parted to permit the entry of his tongue. It found hers and a sweet rush of pleasure melted through her. She ached with arousal. She was trembling with it. "Walker," she muttered . . . but she had no idea what she wanted to say.

Bemused, she drew away slightly and looked into his face. She wished she could see his eyes more clearly so that she could know what he was thinking.

"I want to see you again," he said, his breath warm against her cheek.

"I don't think I can be of any more help with the case, so there's no reason for us to meet again."

For a moment his rugged features fell into an expression of perplexity. Had he expected her to eagerly agree? Was it possible the kiss had plunged him into the same wild sweetness as she? Not likely. He was clearly the far more experienced with members of the opposite sex. What was another kiss to a man like Walker Dietrick?

"On the contrary, honey," he said roughly, "there's more reason than ever now."

Chapter 4

Moonlight spilled through Marty's bedroom window, turning the pale-blue comforter a silver-white. She was sharply aware of the bungalow's settling and creaking, sounds that usually went unnoticed. Now and then, the loose screen on the bathroom window rattled. Like bones, she thought cheerlessly. The wind's velocity had increased during the hour she'd been trying to get to sleep. Its ebb and flow hummed like the unmelodic tunes she'd played as a child by blowing on a comb covered with tissue paper.

Such a melancholy sound, but that was probably her mood, a mood that was uncommon enough to be troubling. She was not ordinarily aware of experiencing loneliness, and had trained herself to be content with her own company. Marty had made a few casual friends in Willow, but no close ones. She hadn't been

conscious of this as a lack in her life. After a very hard
day at work, Marty was usually satisfied to spend her
free evenings at home with needlework, a good book
or professional journal, an occasional TV show. Self-
contained, Jerry had said, and she supposed that described her pretty well. If she was a loner, it was by her
own choice. It was a mistake to depend on other people to make you happy. Happiness came from within,
a lesson she'd learned well during the past two years.

But tonight she was wondering if what she'd been
thinking of as contentment was just existence in a well-
worn rut. Absence of pain was not necessarily happiness. Tonight with Walker she'd felt so vibrantly
aware, as though she'd awakened refreshed from a
prolonged sleep. Walker's parting remark had left her
with an odd shivery feeling, as if there was something
unfinished between them. She didn't think she could
sink back contentedly into her solitude until she knew
whatever it was was ended. The thought made her
smile wryly in the darkness. She was making too much
of the evening. Middle-of-the-night thoughts were always more dramatic than those that came during the
day. Probably because the mind was drifting between
waking and sleeping.

Only, in this case, she was as far from sleep as she'd
been upon coming to bed. Marty had banished Walker from her mind again and again, but he always
came back. Right now she could close her eyes and see
him smile as clearly as though she were still seated
across from him at Emil's Country Inn. Had he really
called her honey? Did he use the term indiscrimi-
nately, or did it mean something special to him? Lord,

what ailed her? She usually disliked men who addressed women they barely knew with such overfamiliar terms. But Walker had made the word sound like a caress....

Restlessly, she shifted on her side, trying to find a position that would induce sleep. It was only a word, she reminded herself, and his kiss had only been a kiss. She had had many in her life. As for Walker, the women he'd kissed could well number in the hundreds. She was a ninny to imagine there had been something singular about this particular one. A man took a woman to dinner, and when he brought her home, he kissed her. It was part of American culture, a social custom.

Everybody did it, for heaven's sake.

Rockets hadn't exploded. The earth hadn't moved— except in her feverish imagination. Old girl, she chided herself, two years is too long between kisses. Maybe she should get out more. She might even consider saying yes the next time Jerry asked her for a date.

She flopped on her back. "Ahh," she muttered. "There's a stupid idea for you." What she didn't need was *two* men trying to do a number on her. She certainly hadn't handled Walker's advances very well tonight. What made her think she'd fare any better with Jerry, Willow's champion ladies' man?

She turned on her side again and punched her pillow. *Go to sleep, Marty.* She was experiencing what one of her clients had called "night creepies," anxious thoughts that bedeviled you when you should be sleeping, but couldn't. The next day you wondered

why everything had seemed so bleak during the night.
Perspective would return with daylight.

Walker wasn't even trying to sleep. He'd called Jess
to report that there was nothing to report. Jess had
insisted that Walker have Sunday lunch with him and
Rose the next day. Not that it had taken much urging.
Walker never turned down an invitation from the
Stouts if he could help it. Since his parents had retired
and moved to Dallas to be near their grandchildren, he
didn't often get good home cooking like Rose's.

After the phone call, Walker planted himself in his
favorite chair in front of the television set. He had sat
through a detective show and half of a John Wayne
movie, but he couldn't have related the plot of either.
His mind was still with Marty Newland.

She hadn't provided any new information in the
Allman case, even though she'd obviously tried. But
then he hadn't really expected anything to come of
their little experiment. He'd gone to her house at Jess's
instruction and against his better judgment. Maybe it
had been above and beyond the call of duty to take her
to dinner and for a drive afterward. But kissing
her . . . well, that had nothing to do with duty. That he
had done simply because he'd wanted to—since the
first time he'd seen her.

He'd been trying to separate the case and her claim
to precognition from his personal feelings about Marty
ever since he got home. It wasn't easy. She wasn't like
any woman he'd ever known before.

Once more, he listed the pertinent facts gleaned
from the evening spent with her. She wasn't a fraud or

a nut. She truly believed in the existence of ESP, and she was convinced she was blessed—or cursed—with it. She definitely had some experiences that were hard to explain, and from what she'd said he thought they'd brought her more pain than happiness. That being the case, she had no stake in deliberately inducing the precognitive incidents as far as he could see. So they weren't under her conscious control. She became defensive when confronted with disbelief; his suggestion that she try to get a feeling about one of the houses they drove past had definitely made her uncomfortable. Given the attitude of her parents, her sensitivity to doubt was understandable.

Since the experiences were hers, she could hardly be objective about them. Walker could be, and he still leaned toward the opinion that Marty's dreams and "hunches" could be explained without resorting to the paranormal. She wasn't consciously faking herself out, but the human brain was a mysterious organ, the function of which nobody fully understood. Take what happened when she was nine years old. Her grandfather's picture fell and she had a sudden conviction he was "in trouble." Kids can be superstitious. Maybe she'd seen a movie or heard a story in which something similar happened. She might not consciously remember it, but her subconscious could have made the connection. In which case, her grandfather's heart attack three hours later was the "coincidence" her parents had insisted it was.

As for Julia Allman, Marty had admitted that she could have seen her previously and forgotten it. Even if she hadn't known about the kidnapping before the dream, she knew what had happened to Linda Niles. Julia Allman was a Willow State student, the same as the Niles girl. If Marty had seen Julia recently, wasn't it possible that's the only connection her subconscious needed to construct the dream? If that's what happened, then the timing of Julia's abduction was another "coincidence."

And maybe that was as farfetched as the ESP explanation. Coincidence, after all, was what you called something you couldn't otherwise explain.

Grunting, Walker got to his feet and went to the kitchen for a beer. He sat at the kitchen table, drinking from the chilled can. He was impatient with mental mazes like the ones his mind had been following the past two hours. He dealt with acts and overt consequences. Written laws and precedents. Law abiders and lawbreakers. Legal accountability and punishment. The complete psychological skein of motives in most cases was impossible to untangle, and he didn't try. He left that to the psychiatrists and psychologists. If they said a perpetrator was capable of knowing right from wrong when he committed a crime, that's all Walker needed to know to build a case for a prosecutor to take to the jury.

But he was too damned attracted to Marty to write off what she insisted was ESP without second thoughts. He wanted to keep on seeing her—a lot. But he didn't think she would let herself get very close to anyone who doubted the genuineness of her precognition. She was too sensitive about it to be able to keep it separate from other aspects of a relationship.

He finished the beer, tossed the can into the trash, and headed for the bathroom. Maybe a hot shower would relax him and he could get some sleep. He was accomplishing nothing by chasing his thoughts in endless circles.

Everything else aside, he was going to see Marty again—one way or another.

Marty awoke very early the next morning tangled in the bedclothes. One moment she was asleep, the next moment she was wide awake, her heart racing. In a claustrophobic panic, she struggled with the covers until she was free of them.

Her panic slowly receding, she sat up. She'd dreamed about Julia Allman again. The dream was the same in every detail as the previous one.

This was extraordinary. She couldn't ever remember having the same precognitive experience twice. Was there any special significance in the repetition?

She didn't know.

Certain she wouldn't be able to go back to sleep, Marty put on robe and slippers and went to the kitchen to make a pot of coffee. It was Sunday and she had no plans. After such an unpropitious beginning to the day, the hours were sure to drag.

Since she'd readied the percolator the night before, she merely plugged it into the electric outlet and sat down at the table to wait. But the urgency left over from the dream was still with her, and she couldn't keep still. She rose to wander about the kitchen. Why did she have the dream a second time? Did it mean that Julia Allman's situation had become even more dangerous—or soon would? Marty felt she must do something, but what?

Should she call Walker? Maybe he could think of something else to do—if she could somehow impress him with her sense of urgency. She made herself wait until ten o'clock to phone. While she waited, she did her laundry and fixed a couple of casseroles for the coming week, storing them in the freezer.

When she dialed, Walker didn't answer. She called the police station and was told Walker wasn't expected all day. She phoned his house every hour after that until four o'clock when she gave up in discouragement. Maybe he'd left town for the day, or was spending it with friends. Was he with a woman? That was a disturbing thought and she pushed it away.

Another restless night renewed her decision to reach Walker. She decided to try as soon as she got to the clinic. When she walked in, Dotty was talking on the telephone. She looked up, said, "Just a minute," and covered the receiver with her hand. "Marty," she called, "this is for you."

Shrugging off her jacket in her office, Marty held the receiver between chin and shoulder. "Marty Newland speaking."

"Hi."

The deep voice made a honeylike sweetness spread through her body. Smiling, she tossed her jacket aside and lowered herself slowly into a chair. Her fingers curled about the hard, cool plastic of the receiver.

"Hello, Walker. I was going to call you."

"You were?" Somehow she knew he was grinning.

She swallowed. "I tried to reach you yesterday and couldn't."

"Ah, I wish I'd known. I had an early lunch with Chief Stout and his wife, and then spent the afternoon at the college library."

That made her laugh. "Why can't I imagine you spending the afternoon in a library?"

"I guess you don't see me as the intellectual type." He chuckled deep in his throat.

"Well... I see you more as a man of action. Tell me, what were you doing at the college library?"

"Not ogling the pretty girls, if that's what you think."

She laughed again. "How did you know?"

"It follows. You've got me pegged as a skirt chaser."

"Hmm, that may be a bit strong, but not totally off the mark."

He sighed. "I can see I'm going to have to correct a few misconceptions. I went to the library for the obvious reason. I needed to do some reading."

She pictured Walker sprawled at a library table, his long legs extended, head bent over a book, auburn hair falling across his forehead, and her face took on a rapt expression. "Were you doing research for a case?"

"In a way. I read everything they had on ESP."

She felt ridiculously pleased. "Did you reach any conclusions?"

"I found out some people with pretty impressive credentials are involved in the research." What had she expected—you win, Marty, I'm convinced?

"That's a start," she murmured.

"I told you I'm reserving judgment, Marty."

She coiled the phone cord around her finger and leaned back in her chair. "I think we've gotten off the track. Why did you call?"

"After the other night, do you really have to ask?"

This is happiness, she thought, this glowing lightness trickling through her like liquid sunshine. She would have liked to touch him then. "Walker," she said, sobering and feeling the glow leave her. "I had the dream again Saturday night."

"That's why you wanted to talk to me yesterday?"

"Yes. I was frightened. I've never before had the same dream twice."

"Why do you think you did this time?"

Was there, after all, any significance in the repetition of the dream? What did she have to go on but a hunch? When the silence became uncomfortable, she said, "I think that girl is in terrible danger. Even more than before. I tried to reach you because I had to tell somebody."

"I'm sorry I wasn't there when you needed me."

"It's okay. You can't do much about it, anyway, right?"

"We're haunting the campus, questioning anybody even remotely connected to Julia Allman or Linda Niles. Unless we turn up something new, I don't know where we go from there."

"I wish I could do something." Her voice trembled.

"I know." There was a pause. Then he said, "I have to see you, Marty. Will you have dinner with me tonight?"

"And drive around looking at houses again? Oh, Walker, if you're hoping—"

He interrupted, "I thought we'd drive to Altus. It would probably do us both some good to get out of town for a while."

He wanted nothing from her then except her company. She didn't even hesitate. "You're so right. I'd like to go to Altus with you."

"Is seven okay?"

"Perfect."

"Good, I'll see you then. And, honey, try not to worry too much."

Jerry wandered into Marty's office after her first counseling session of the day. "Dotty said Walker Dietrick called here again." He sucked on his pipe. "What is it with that guy?"

Marty glanced up from the notes she was making. "He's working on a case."

"The coed's disappearance?"

"Yes."

"What does that have to do with you?"

"Nothing directly."

"What does it have to do with you even indirectly?"

"It's rather involved, Jerry—"

"Your attitude toward the guy seems to have changed."

Marty's telephone rang and she reached for it. "I don't have time to talk about it now."

After staring at her for a moment, he left, shaking his head.

The trip to Altus, as Walker had predicted, was a relaxing diversion. For a little while, Marty managed to forget Julia Allman and the dreams. Walker told her about his family—his parents, two married sisters, and five nieces and nephews. They had all moved away from Willow and now lived in the Dallas area.

"I miss having them around," Walker said. "Even when I didn't get by to see them for days at a time, I knew they were there." They had finished a lobster dinner and were lingering over the last of a bottle of Chablis. "We talk on the telephone a couple of times a month, but it's not the same."

"If you're raised in a close family, I guess it's like losing a limb when you're separated. I wouldn't know from personal experience. You can't miss what you never had." Too late, Marty wondered if her words sounded self-pitying. She hadn't meant them to. She smiled to take the gravity out of her revelation. "Being an only child is the pits."

"Yeah, I want two kids, at least."

Marty gave him an arch look. "Preceded by a wedding ceremony, I trust."

He grinned boyishly. "Naturally. I'm a very conservative guy."

Marty thought about that conversation as they were driving back to Willow. After Walker had phoned her at the clinic that morning, Dotty, who knew all the local gossip, had taken it upon herself to tell Marty about the numerous women Walker had courted over the past ten years. None of them had lasted very long, Dotty said. It was Dotty's opinion that Walker was too particular, and the longer he remained a bachelor, the more particular he would get. Marty suspected Dotty's words were meant to warn her, in case she was becoming interested in Walker. But underneath Walker's love-'em-and-leave-'em image, he was an old-fashioned man. He just hadn't found the right woman yet. What she must do, Marty thought, was keep reminding herself that she wasn't the right woman, either. She and Walker were too different. Opposites might attract, but they usually had a terrible time trying to live together.

Where in the world had the thought of living with Walker come from? She was a private person who valued her solitude. The wine must have addled her. When they got into the car, Walker had pulled her close to his side and reached for her hand. The slow strains of a romantic song floated from the car radio. Captured beneath his big hand, hers now lay curled against his knee. It felt good.

Walker was a toucher. Touching was as natural to him as breathing. When they walked side by side, he always settled his hand against the small of her back or put his arm around her shoulders. Driving in the car, he held her hand. The only reason she was in danger of giving this more importance than it merited was that she had grown up in a household where touching was rare. It was okay to like his touch, she told herself, as long as she didn't start needing it too much. Need was the enemy, so she'd better pull herself out of this dreamy fog before she lost her way.

To break the spell being woven by the music, she asked, "Have you come up with any new leads in the Allman case?"

He stirred, as though he had been caught up in the yearning love song, and threaded his fingers through hers on his knee. "We're keeping her boyfriend under surveillance but, so far, there's nothing."

She stared at him. "The paper didn't say anything about a boyfriend."

"I don't think it's a serious relationship. It's just that she dated this Greg Grimes more than anybody else. He doesn't seem to be involved in Julia's disappearance, but we have to be sure."

"He's a student at the college?"

He nodded. "A senior." He glanced at her and squeezed her hand. "Let's not spoil a lovely evening by talking about the case."

She put her head back against the seat. "You're right. It will only depress us."

They passed a farm Walker recognized, and he said, "That's Dave Guinn's place. He used to grow the best watermelons around here. When I was in high school, one of the rites of passage was that you had to swipe a melon from Guinn's patch. One night I came out here with two of my buddies..."

He was trying to take her mind off the case. Marty closed her eyes and listened to the deep cadence of his voice as he described the raid on Guinn's watermelon patch, how the farmer's dogs chased them. They barely got away with the seats of their pants intact, but were clutching three melons that proved their manhood.

Before he was through, Marty was laughing with him. She opened her eyes and watched him. They had entered the outskirts of Willow and light from the street lamps glinted on the waves of his dark red hair and thick lashes. Her throat tightened achingly. He was beautiful, she thought, not like a matinee idol or in any classic sense, but as a man should be. He reminded her of the bronze statues she had seen in parks, so strong and heroic. At some essential level, she had always been awed by those statues. Watching Walker laugh with the light playing off the manly angles of his face moved her in the same way, and her heart constricted.

She wasn't surprised when he drove to his house. He should have taken me home, she thought. But that deep part of her that admired bronze statues was glad that he hadn't.

His house was the old-fashioned kind with a screened porch in front and big rooms. "I bought it from my folks when they decided to move," he said, leading her into the living room. He took her jacket and folded it over the back of the Boston rocker.

She liked the comfortably worn furniture in shades of brown and green, the gleaming oak floor with a braided rag rug defining a conversational area flanked by a sofa and two roomy overstuffed armchairs. "It's so clean."

He came up behind her and placed his hands on her shoulders. "I was going to point that out to you if you didn't notice. I spent two hours this afternoon getting it this way."

She turned to look up at him, smiling. "You cleaned house just for me?"

"Just for you." She watched the play of muscle under the skin of his face as he spoke, yearning to run her fingers through the thick sweep of hair on his forehead. She felt as though an invisible force flowed through their bodies, connecting them. She gazed into the depths of his hazel eyes and felt drugged and dreamy, wondering whether, if she closed her eyes and opened them again, he would be gone.

The silence seemed fraught with exposed emotions, quivering like raw nerve endings. "You are so lovely," he said and took her in his arms.

His kiss was like plunging into a clear blue pool from a seared landscape. She was hungry for it, and her need for his touch had built to a crescendo. She felt like an empty receptacle so deep it could never be filled. Where he touched her, it felt as though the heat of his hand melted her skin and he made contact with the blood and marrow. Marty imagined crazily that his touch could penetrate deeply enough to grasp her soul.

Never had she known such need. Instead of a placid pool, she had plunged into a raging torrent. One didn't expect to step unscathed from such a churning flood, but could only hope to keep head above water.

She was trembling as her arms found their way around his strong neck. His arms encircled her and tightened. The kiss grew desperate. Her palms pressed against the corded muscles at the back of his neck, and his hands moved convulsively, one to cup her hip, the other to tangle in her hair.

The soul-deep ache of her need made her press her body against him with an urgency that staggered them both. Walker tore his mouth from hers and, taking deep, ragged breaths, buried his face in her silken hair. In a hoarse, compelling voice, he whispered, "My God, Marty!"

He touched her cheek as though to assure himself that she was real. After a moment, he drew back only enough to look down at her. She felt a tremor in his fingers. "I've never needed anyone like this," he said huskily. "Let me love you, honey."

There was a long pause. Marty closed her eyes and tried to make sense of what was happening. The heat of his body pressing against hers burned through her clothes and her lips felt bruised from his kiss, but it was a sweet bruising and she wanted more. She knew all the reasons why she should say no, but reason was a frail opponent for the desire she had just experienced, was still experiencing. At such moments of high emotion—when one is least able to think of consequences—life-altering decisions are made. She opened her eyes and looked into his rugged face, her lips softening and parting.

"I want you," she murmured simply and with three words exposed the part of herself that she had sworn never to show anyone again.

Chapter 5

Walker had been kissing her for hours, it seemed, but she didn't think she could ever get enough. Through a soft, erotic haze, she thought, I want him to go on kissing me forever. There was a languor in her limbs that made her weak. "I feel as though I'm going to fall," she whispered against his searching lips.

"I won't let you," he said, the words so unsteady it surprised and touched the deepest part of her with wonder. In one easy, graceful movement, Walker scooped her up into his arms and carried her to his bed.

He laid her gently down and half-reclined beside her. The room was muted with indirect light from the living room. He cradled her head in his hands and began to brush tender kisses on her brow and in the hollows of her cheeks. Lifting a languid hand, she cupped the back of his neck and murmured, "Walker," half pleading, half inviting.

He lifted his head and looked down at her, a fierce masculine need darkening his pupils, as though the mere sight of her stirred him incredibly. Scintillating tremors, like tiny shock waves, traveled all over her skin, beginning in her stomach and running outward to her hands and feet. Her fingers traced the bones surrounding his eye and then his cheek. The sensitive pads of her fingers aroused her anew. I must touch him everywhere, she thought with exquisite pleasure at the prospect. The look in his eyes tugged at the sensuous core of her, and when his strong hand caressed her cheek she turned her head to place a moist kiss in his palm. Inside her a fire such as she had never known had been kindled. She wondered distantly if it was possible for a person to burn from the inside.

Under his gaze, she felt her nipples contract painfully. She shivered and he lowered his eyes, seeing the evidence of her arousal through her lace bra and the clinging fabric of her blouse. When his eyes returned to her face, they were filled with a desperate longing.

She looked at him, her lovely, haunting eyes glazed and velvet-soft. "Walker," she said, her voice breaking because she was suddenly fearful, "wait." But his hands were already unbuttoning her blouse and the waistband of her skirt, and she knew it would be the worst kind of treachery to change her mind now. Anyway, she couldn't.

She didn't think he had even heard her, for he undressed her with quick efficiency, then stood beside the bed to strip himself. Her breath caught in her throat as he dropped his briefs. Their eyes took each other in greedily, and his sharp intake of breath was loud in the silence. Her tongue moistened her parted lips and she swallowed the unexpected clump of tears in her throat.

He dropped to the bed beside her, his eyes holding hers. She ran her hand along the rippling muscles of his upper arm. "I'm afraid I won't please you," she admitted.

"Ah, sweetheart, there's no danger of that." His hungry mouth came down on her parted lips, swallowing her deep moan of feminine need.

Her fingers explored the taut male body that covered her, everywhere she could reach: the broad, muscled shoulders, the smooth hardness at the small of his back, the lean buttocks. "Your body is so beautiful and exciting to me," she whispered with breathless wonder.

With a low groan, he burrowed into the side of her neck to inhale her sweet fragrance and taste her creamy skin. Plunging her fingers into his thick, wavy hair she threw her head back, offering her throat to his devouring kisses.

He shifted to dip his head lower and brand her hardened nipples with his tongue. The rasping strokes electrified her, and her body moved restlessly, arching to meet him. Glorying in the excitement that raced through her, she was bathed in hot, sensual awareness. Flooded by sensation, she was only half conscious of her own murmurs of pleasure.

Reveling in her passionate response, Walker's tongue moistened her navel, and then he moved lower still to feather kisses across the slight concavity of her stomach and the softness of her inner thighs.

She felt the heat of his breath on her skin, and she began to tremble. Never in all her life had she experienced such a profoundly sensual response. His hands and mouth set her skin on fire, and when his fingers stroked the burning core of her, she began to shudder uncontrollably.

She let out a desperate moan that told him what his touch was doing to her. She felt that her whole life had been nothing until this moment, that this man had succeeded in unlocking the deepest secrets of her soul where all others had failed, that she had been made for this. And then the spasms rose in her and the sweet release poured out of her, leaving her trembling helplessly but free in a way that she could not explain.

When he looked into her eyes, she felt tears start. She smiled at him through a misty veil. She touched him and when she felt his shuddering response, she caressed him. Then, because in that moment she could tell him anything, she said, "I want to feel you inside me."

With a harsh gasp, he knelt above her, the indistinct light gilding his body so that, for an instant, he reminded her again of a bronze statue. Her arms reached out to enclose him, and she felt the heat and faint moisture of his skin and the momentary illusion was shattered.

He slid inside her, then buried his face in her neck and groaned as he fought back the racking spasms. He lifted his head and his hands caressed her hair.

"There's no other woman in the world like you, Marty, love." He began to move in her, slow, satiny strokes.

"I never knew it could be like this, Walker," she whispered softly. "I never knew."

He kissed her with passionate abandon, gasping guttural words against her lips. "Oh, Marty, honey!"

Her hand pressed against his back, feeling the ripple of his muscles, and she felt her body begin a second climb. Her body followed the movement of his, her hands spread on the small of his back, urging him deeper and deeper within her. A deep growl of ecstasy escaped him and his body convulsed at the same moment that she felt herself plunging over the edge, her response even more shattering than before.

She muffled her cry of surprise against his damp shoulder.

Marty lay curled against Walker's side, cozy in the shelter of his arms. Wordlessly he stroked her back, and she felt the gentlest of kisses on her hair. Her eyelids drooped in the most total contentment she had ever known. For the first time in her life, she understood what it was to be one with another person. She knew this complete joining of her heart and soul with his would forever be a part of her, no matter what the future held.

Minutes later, she stretched and lifted her head to rest her chin in her hand. "I've been thinking, Walker."

A slow smile spread over his face, the flame rekindling in his eyes. He curled his hand about the back of her neck. "So have I." He pulled her down for his kiss.

She relaxed against him for a moment before she blinked and raised herself on her elbow again. "I wasn't thinking about that."

"You wound me." He tugged a lock of her hair. "What then?"

"I want to help on the Allman case."

"You mean drive around town again?"

She shook her head. "No. I want to get a look at Greg Grimes. Maybe I'll be able to tell if he's the man in my dream."

"We'd have to bring him to the station. We don't even want him to know we're watching him, Marty."

She was disappointed, but Walker's reluctance didn't change her mind. Somehow she had to get a look at Grimes.

"Well, then do you think you could bring me something that belonged to Julia, a piece of costume jewelry or clothing?"

He looked away from her. "I thought you said you're not clairvoyant."

"Before Saturday night, I'd never tried to be. It might not work, but isn't it worth a try?"

He placed the tip of his finger under her chin. "We agreed not to talk about this tonight."

His expression told her everything she needed to know, and the oneness she had been feeling cracked. She felt so let down she almost sobbed. All the reading he had done at the library hadn't changed his mind about her. He still wasn't convinced her extrasensory experiences were anything but delusion. And she had been so sure she could trust him. She had opened herself to him, given herself so completely. . . .

She slid from the bed and began to gather up her discarded clothing.

Walker sat up in bed, watching her and scowling. "What are you doing?"

"I'm going home." She located the final item of clothing and started for the bathroom. Behind her, she heard Walker scrambling from the bed.

"Marty. . ."

She stepped into the bathroom and closed the door. She tried not to look at herself in the mirror as she dressed. What a fool she had been. Would she ever learn to judge men realistically?

Ten minutes later she came out of the bathroom, fully dressed even to her jacket. Walker had put on his jeans and was sitting on the side of the bed, waiting for her. "Is all this because I don't want to talk about the case?"

She looked at his bare chest, the triangle of dark red hair that tapered to the snap fastening of his jeans. Dear God, he was breathtaking. She turned away from him to pick up her purse. "I just want to go home, Walker. If you'd rather not go out again, I can walk. It's only a few blocks."

He heaved an exasperated sigh. "No, damn it, you won't walk. I'll be ready in a minute."

She went into the living room to wait for him.

"Afterward, he always seems so sorry." Fern Small had been talking for a half hour about the abusive man she was living with. "I think he really means it, too."

"What I'm hearing, Fern, is that he operates by a predictable pattern. First he starts an argument, then he hits you or threatens to leave you, and once you've stopped disagreeing with him and started to cry, he apologizes."

Fern's hand fluttered above her stiffly sprayed hairdo. She'd been to the beauty shop since her last visit. Fern's natural salt-and-pepper hair was more flattering with her sharp features than the coal-black crown she now wore. The dye job was another desperate attempt to remain young looking and attractive to men.

"Are you saying he's not really sorry even though he says he is?"

"No, I'm not saying that. He probably is sorry right at that moment. But he doesn't feel bad enough to alter his behavior the next time, does he?"

Fern frowned and sighed heavily. "He just can't help it, I guess."

Marty let the silence linger for several moments before she said, "You know, Fern, when people continue to act in the same way, again and again, it usually means the behavior is getting them something they want."

Fern examined her long, scarlet nails. "You mean he wants me to cry? I don't get it."

"Think about it for a minute."

After a long pause, Fern said tentatively, "Could it be he needs to be sure I still want him...even when he hurts me?"

Marty was pleased with this rare bit of insight. "Could be. Why don't you try walking away the next time he tries to start an argument. Go for a drive and give him time to cool off. See what happens when you come back."

"What if he still wants to pick a fight?"

"You can always refuse to be baited. Tell him calmly that you don't want to argue. If he threatens to leave, tell him that's a decision he'll have to make for himself."

Forgetting her fresh manicure, Fern chewed a thumbnail.

"I'm not sure you understand how much I need him, Miss Newland." She looked up and giggled like a schoolgirl. "I'm not worth shooting when I don't have a man around. Charley has his faults but he sure knows how to make a woman feel special in bed."

"If you're willing to put up with his abuse just to keep him around, it'll go on happening."

Fern stuck out her bottom lip. "I guess you think I don't have much pride."

"It's what you think that's important, Fern." Marty glanced at her watch. It was noon. "We'll talk about that next time. Think about bringing this up in the group."

"Oh, I couldn't!"

"It's only a suggestion. You do what you feel comfortable with."

After Fern left, Marty got a sandwich, fruit and thermos of milk she'd brought from home. While she ate at her desk, she continued to think about the session with Fern. From what Fern had said, the only part of her relationship with her current boyfriend that was any good was the sex. Fern seemed willing to excuse a lot of unpleasantness in exchange for that.

Marty remembered how Walker had made her feel the previous night, and she understood Fern's attitude a little better than she had before. The clinic was quiet, both Jerry and Dotty having gone out for lunch. Marty tried pushing away the memories all morning, but they flooded in on her now in the stillness.

The feel of Walker's touch, the weight of his body on hers, the low rumble of his sweet words in her ear, were almost as real as they had been the night before. She suddenly felt flushed and, sighing, realized that the risk of losing moments like that might be one Fern could not take.

She didn't want to be another Fern Small, dependent on a man for her self-esteem. It wasn't enough to have good sex with a man. There had to be trust and faith in the relationship or it was self-destructive. Walker had no faith in her. His reluctance to discuss the Julia Allman case last night proved he didn't believe she could be of any help to him. She would be better off if she never saw Walker Dietrick again. But when she thought about not seeing him, she felt as though a small hand squeezed her heart.

That night she went to the campus to teach Jerry's psychology class, arriving early enough to stop at the college library. The feeling that she should be doing something to help find Julia Allman had been with her all day. Since she had no idea what to do, she had decided to look through the college yearbook for the man in her dream. She realized it was a long shot, but it was better than doing nothing.

The yearbooks, one for each year since the college had started publishing them in 1932, were stored with the reserve collection in the basement. It was quiet there, with only a few students scattered about the room at the long tables.

Marty found the previous year's book and sat at an unoccupied table to leaf through it. She turned first to the pictures of last year's junior class and found Greg Grimes, the young man Walker had said the police were keeping under surveillance. It was a sharp photograph. Greg Grimes wore a sober expression on his thin face, a shock of blond hair brushed smoothly across his forehead. It was impossible to tell his height from the picture, of course, but he looked quite thin. Even though she had seen the man in her dream only from the back, she had seen enough to know that Greg Grimes was not that man. She studied the photograph for several moments, wondering if Greg Grimes loved Julia. If he did, he must have been going through hell since her disappearance.

Checking her watch, she saw that she still had time to spare before the class. She turned to the front of the yearbook and slowly turned the pages, scanning male faces. She found several photographs that could be of the man in her dream, but she had no feeling about any of them. She would, she realized, have to see the man in person to be able to identify him. Even then, she might not be sure since she hadn't seen his face. Discouraged, she returned the yearbook to the shelf and went to teach the class.

The campus was fairly well lighted, but as Marty crossed the oval green that the older classroom buildings faced, she found herself looking for dark corners where a man could hide. There were any number of them. She passed no one as she hurried to the Social Science Building. It would be a simple matter, she realized, for a man to hide in waiting for a woman walking alone and drag her into the shadows. She reminded herself that Julia Allman had disappeared in broad daylight, but it didn't erase her fear. She was practically running by the time she reached the wide steps leading to the brightly lighted entrance. She ran up and pushed through the heavy glass doors, pausing just inside to catch her breath.

She hadn't realized it was such a long walk from where she had left her car. Perhaps it only seemed long because she had made herself anxious by thinking about the kidnapped women. She would leave the building with her students, she decided. Maybe some of them would be going in her direction.

She climbed the stairs to the second floor. Several classes were already in session. She heard a professor's droning voice from one room and, from another, the sound of group laughter in response to something the teacher said. In such surroundings, the possibility of foul play seemed farfetched. Shaking her head over her self-induced agitation a few minutes earlier, she went along the hall to the correct classroom. She was ten minutes early. Time to glance over her notes one more time.

At ten minutes after eight, it was clear that almost half the students enrolled in the class weren't coming.

"They must have heard there was a substitute," Marty joked.

"There's a big Halloween party over at the Union tonight," a male student told her.

A young woman in the first row shook her head and said gravely, "That's not it, Miss Newland. They're afraid to walk across campus at night. I don't blame them. If I didn't have Tom here to walk me to and from class, I wouldn't have come, either."

"We're going around in groups, even in daylight," said another girl. "My mother wants me to come home until they find the maniac who took Linda and Julia."

A male voice from the back of the room said, "That might take years. You can't hide for the rest of your life."

"Yeah, there's no absolute safety anywhere," said another young man. "You could choke on a piece of meat or fall down the stairs and break your neck in your own house."

"You guys are really cheering us up," chided the girl in the front row.

"They've got a weird sense of humor," said another girl.

"Speaking of which," Marty interjected, "our topic for tonight is abnormal psychology." This got a laugh from the students. "Who wants to tell us the difference between a psychosis and a neurosis?"

Soon all of the students were participating in a lively and penetrating discussion. Pleased with the way the class was going, Marty forgot her apprehension about walking back to her car alone—until she dismissed the class and followed a group of students outside, only to see them walk in the opposite direction from hers. Standing on the bottom step, she buttoned her coat against the wind and watched the departing students disappear into the darkness beyond the green.

"Marty."

She whirled around to see Walker striding toward her along one of the paved walkways. He was wearing a sheepskin jacket, jeans and cowboy boots.

"What are you doing here?"

"I phoned the clinic and got the answering service. They told me where you were." He reached her and, grasping her arms, steadied her as she stepped off the last step to the ground. "I was worried about you walking around out here alone." His hands on her arms tightened. "You're shaking. What's wrong?"

She had never been so happy to see anyone in her life. "Nothing. I—just didn't realize the campus would be so deserted." Impulsively she stepped closer until their bodies were touching. "Oh, Walker, am I glad to see you!"

He hugged her tightly, and she pressed against him. He made her feel so safe. "Where did you leave your car?" He spoke into her hair.

"In the south lot."

"Come on. I'll walk you there, and then I'll go get my car and follow you home."

She tilted her head back to look up at him. "Oh, you don't have to do that. If you'll just see me to my car, I'll be fine."

Tucking her shoulder beneath his arm, he started walking across the green. "I'll follow you home," he repeated, and she realized that he wanted to go home with her. It wasn't only that he feared for her safety. It was impossible to say no when he had his arm around her so protectively.

When she was in her car, driving toward the bungalow, she told herself she would send him away at her door. She had been over and over it today, and she knew it was best to stop seeing Walker. They were not well suited. The relationship could go nowhere. But from a corner of her brain came the question, Would it hurt to let him come inside for a few minutes? Turning into her own driveway, she still had not found a completely satisfactory answer to the question.

Walker didn't give her any more time to ponder. Bounding onto the porch behind her, he took the key from her hand and opened the door. He stepped inside and found the light switch.

Marty slipped out of her coat and took it to the hall closet. She didn't know Walker had followed her until she turned around and was gathered into his arms.

Overwhelmed by the smell and warmth of him, she buried her face in the hollow of his neck and let him hold her for a moment. God, it felt good. Erotic images of their lovemaking the previous night flashed through her mind, and the heaviness of need made her feel suddenly too weighted to move. How had he become so necessary to her in such a short time? Oh, she needed him!

But she couldn't need him. Tears of regret filled her closed eyes. She had to fight this dependence that threatened to wreck her self-sufficiency.

Blinking away her tears, she lifted her head. She forced her voice past the tightness in her throat. "You must go now. Thank you for seeing me home."

His jaw tightened, and she could feel the tension humming in his body. When she would have turned away from him, he grabbed her shoulders and hauled her back. "We have to talk about last night," he said with sudden harshness.

She bent her head to hide her face behind the fall of her hair. "No," she whispered, "I don't want to."

"Why?" He gripped her chin between his thumb and forefinger and forced her to look at him. "It was too soon, wasn't it? I rushed you. I'm sorry."

"No, it's more than that.... Please, don't say any more."

"Why can't we talk about it?"

She stared at him, striving for calm. "Talking won't change what happened. The less said about it, the better."

He took a deep breath. "Are you sorry it happened?" He sounded angry and incredulous.

"Yes," she whispered.

"I don't believe you," he growled and covered her mouth fiercely with his own. In that first hot instant, before she slid into the sensuous depths of the kiss, she tried to turn her head away. His hand moved to cup her head, and his other arm wrapped her tightly. His jacket was open, and her breasts pressed against him. She could feel a tremor in his arms and hands and body, and a flood of desire swamped her.

At last he lifted his head and looked down into her eyes. "Can you actually stand there and tell me you didn't love last night as much as I did?"

She was burning up with the memory of last night, of how desperate and helpless his touch had made her. She had to get free of this hold he had on her. . . .

She swallowed convulsively. "No." She lifted a shaking hand to her cheek and swallowed again. "But I can't let it happen again, knowing what you think of me." This time when she pulled away, he let her go. On unsteady legs, she walked away from him.

He followed her to the living room. "What do you mean? I don't know what you're talking about."

Groping behind her with her hand, she slowly lowered herself into a chair. "I went to the college library earlier this evening. I looked up Greg Grimes's picture in the yearbook. He's not the man I saw in my dream, Walker."

He shook his head, as if confused by the change of subject. "You're sure?"

"Absolutely." She looked up at him expectantly. "What do you want me to say, Marty?"

"Do you intend to keep following Grimes?"

"Yes."

"After what I just said . . ."

He made a deep sound of frustration in his throat. "Marty, listen to me. A vague hunch isn't enough to warrant calling off the surveillance. Besides, when that decision is made, it'll be Chief Stout who makes it."

A vague hunch! That's what he thought of her opinion! "There, you see! You don't believe me. I was a fool to think you'd changed."

In answer, he leaned down, braced his hands against the arms of her chair and kissed her throat and her neck as though the taste of her was sustenance to him. "Don't be so unreasonable," he whispered hoarsely. "I want to make love to you, Marty." His mouth moved over her skin, scorching her.

Her breath escaped in a moan as a battle between panic and desire was joined inside her. "No... Stop..." she gasped, breathless and frightened by how easily he could demolish her resolution.

"Do you really mean it?" he queried huskily as he lifted his mouth from her throat and waited.

"Yes," she managed.

He straightened then, his intent gaze electrifying her, and she knew that this was the man she had waited for all her life, without even being aware of it. She wrenched her gaze from his and looked down at her hand, which lay curled, palm-up on her lap.

Abruptly, he pushed something into her hand. "It's Julia Allman's." With that, he left her.

After she heard the front door closing behind him, she slowly uncurled her fingers. A brown plastic hair clasp lay in her palm.

He slumped against the door, trembling violently. Cold sweat beaded his forehead. He wasn't sure how it had happened. He'd brought her dinner down, a peanut butter sandwich and two oranges. He'd felt pleased with himself because that afternoon he'd remembered how much Rita liked oranges. He'd made a special trip to the supermarket to buy them. Just to please her.

He'd hidden the oranges behind his back as he entered the basement. She'd been sitting on the cot, wedged into the angle of two walls. She'd looked at him dully as he approached. Standing in front of her, he'd presented the oranges with a flourish, hoping for a smile.

She pushed herself off the cot so fast, it was a moment before he understood what she was doing. In that moment, she was past him and flying up the stairs. He caught her at the top, barely an instant before she reached the back door.

There was no moon tonight. If she had thrown open the door and run into the yard . . .

When he caught her, she screamed, a high, shrill keening that made his body hair stand on end. Clamping his arm around her neck, he cut off her air and dragged her down the stairs. He flung her on the cot and she lay limp and unmoving. He thought he'd killed her. He held his shaking hand in front of her face and felt her warm breath and almost fainted with relief. He'd backed up to the door and tried to figure out where he'd miscalculated. He'd been so sure he was winning her over.

On the stairs, when she started screaming, he'd thought: She's not Rita! It was something about the way she looked at him with her mouth open and her eyes wide. For a moment she had looked so different, not like Rita at all. That's when rage had exploded in him and he'd lost contact with himself, grabbed her around the neck and hauled her back like a sack of grain, her shoes thudding against each step on the way down.

Watching the fluttering rise and fall of her chest, he willed his slamming heart to be calm. Everything was all right now. She was Rita—of course, she was. It was just that, in the first place, he hadn't expected her to have forgotten him. In the second place, he'd counted on her realizing who he was before now. He wondered how much longer it would take for her to remember.

She opened her eyes and brought her hand to her throat. She swallowed, grimacing.

"You shouldn't have tried to run away."

She looked at him listlessly. "Please, let me go," she whispered, her voice cracking. "I'll go crazy if I don't get out of this dark, stinking hole."

"It's only until you remember me and how close we used to be. Then you won't be afraid of me anymore." She continued to stare at him; her expression did not change. "I don't blame you, you know. She must have told you horrible lies about me when I left. The same way she lied to me when she told me you'd died."

"I don't know who you're talking about."

"Mother. She lied to both of us, Rita."

She clutched her small hand into a fist and banged it impotently against the cot. "How many times do I have to tell you? My name is Julia!"

He lunged across the room and bent over her. He shook his fist at her. "Don't lie! Don't be like her!"

She scrambled into the corner again. She was scared, but she didn't flinch. She glared up at him defiantly.

She drew a deep breath. "All right. Obviously, I can't fool you. I'm Rita."

Chapter 6

Marty stared into the darkness. Julia Allman's hair clasp was clutched in her hand. For some time she had been trying to free her mind of the confusion left in Walker's wake. She had wanted him to go, hadn't she? She had told him to go and he had gone, leaving behind him the aching need that his kiss had unleashed in her. A treacherous part of her was disappointed that he had left without trying to change her mind.

Face it, Marty, either way, you would have been unhappy. She exhaled a deep breath and wondered how she had managed to get into such a no-win situation.

"I want to make love to you..." She heard Walker's voice like a whisper that was part of the wind that soughed about the bungalow, a whisper accented by the beating of her heart.

"Get out of my head, Walker," she muttered.

She must think about Julia Allman. She concentrated on remembering the details of the newspaper photograph of the girl. She rubbed her finger over the smooth surface of the hair clasp, holding it first in her right hand, and then in her left, even pressing it hard against her cheek.

But it was futile. She saw nothing, felt nothing about the missing girl. All she was sure of was that Greg Grimes was not involved in her disappearance, and she hadn't even been able to convince Walker of that.

Walker. He had looked incredibly masculine in the boots, thigh-molding jeans, and sheepskin jacket he'd worn this evening. Marty moved restlessly in the bed and remembered how Walker had wrapped her in his arms when he met her on the campus green and how she had pressed against him in her happiness at seeing him.

She fell asleep finally, and the memory of Walker's words and kisses made her dream that he was loving her in her bed in the dark room.

She awoke early, the effects of her dreams lingering for a moment, making her body tingle in the warm cocoon of the bedclothes. She stirred and the hard plastic hair clasp, which she had lost her hold on during the night, gouged her thigh.

She laid the clasp on the nightstand, got up and dressed hurriedly. In the kitchen she made coffee, thinking about the day ahead. She had a group session at nine and four hours scheduled later in the day for individual counseling. The psychiatrist who came to the clinic once a week would be there all afternoon to prescribe medication for the patients who needed it. Marty liked Dr. Faigan, and his afternoons at the clinic usually ended in consultation with Marty and Jerry about current clients. Faigan's psychiatric viewpoint was sometimes helpful and Marty enjoyed the discussions, but it meant she probably wouldn't leave the clinic until seven o'clock.

Sipping a cup of fresh coffee, she put a Danish in the microwave oven. While she waited for the pastry to heat she glanced absently at the calendar tacked to the small corkboard next to the kitchen telephone. The month of October was showing, and it was a moment before she remembered that it was no longer October. She tore off the top page, exposing the calendar for November.

It was, Marty thought, as if a time clock had been set and was ticking off the minutes. Today was November first. Julia Allman could die any time now.

This thought remained at the back of Marty's mind in the days that followed. She lost sleep over it, but there was simply nothing she could do to help Julia. Marty wasn't even sure what she saw in her dreams could be prevented; she'd never before tried to alter a future event. Yet she couldn't shake a feeling of responsibility for the missing girl.

She didn't hear from Walker for several days. Her evenings now felt oddly desolate and aimless, oddly lonely. She thought Walker must have come to the same conclusion as she, that it was best if they didn't see each other. She should be grateful, she told herself, that he wasn't going to pursue her. But she wasn't glad; she was depressed. She tried to convince herself her depression was caused by the fact that Julia hadn't been found. But she knew that wasn't the only reason for her heaviness of mind during the long nights. She ached to see Walker, talk to him, touch him...

He phoned her at home Saturday evening. When she heard his voice, she couldn't speak for a moment because suddenly she had to swallow.

"Marty? Are you there?"

"Yes, of course."

"How are you?"

"I'm fine. Didn't you expect me to be?" The question was sharper than she had intended because all at once she was angry, and she didn't know why. Perhaps because he sounded so calm while she felt as though she might cry.

He responded without heat, "I was hoping you'd missed me a little."

"I've been awfully busy at the clinic, and besides it's only been four days."

"You're counting. That's encouraging."

Marty winced. She couldn't deny the obvious. "Oh, well," she said, for something to say, something to hide her deep confusion, "I guess I remembered because the next morning after you were here, I looked at the calendar and realized it was November first. And today's the fourth, which means Julia Allman no longer has even a month to live."

"Actually, I'm calling about the case."

She felt disappointed and angry with herself because of it. Had she really thought he'd called her because he needed to hear her voice? Had she expected him to ask her out and take her home afterward and make love to her? Idiot! You told him it couldn't happen again.

"The hair clasp didn't help. I'm sorry, Walker. I was so hoping it would."

"Don't let it upset you, honey. You tried."

Silly how his calling her honey made goose bumps rise on her arms. "I took it to bed with me, and I carried it around all day. But I didn't get any feelings at all about Julia."

"Maybe you're trying too hard." She didn't respond, and he continued, "The chief wants to meet you."

"Chief Stout wants to meet *me*?"

"Yeah, you're invited to his house for dinner tomorrow night. I've been assigned to get you there."

She wasn't comfortable with the idea of going to the Stout home. Why did they want her there? Were they curious to meet somebody who claimed to have ESP? She'd feel like a freak in a sideshow.

"I don't think I want to go."

"You'll like Jess and Rose, Marty. They're good people."

"I think it's odd that they'd invite a stranger into their home for dinner. It's because of my dream, isn't it?"

"Yes," he admitted, "but they won't insist on talking about it if it makes you uncomfortable. Just remember that Julia's time is running out." Did that mean he'd decided to give her dreams some credence? Or was he merely repeating what she'd said to get his way? He added quietly, "I want to see you, Marty. Please come."

He knew exactly what to say to overcome her reservations. He could have said that in the beginning and spared himself the necessity of explaining. It didn't matter that she resented Chief Stout's curiosity; she would be with Walker. "Promise we can leave when I want to."

"Anything you say, sweetheart."

He sounded so humble it made her want to laugh. He knew how to get around her objections, all right. She smiled, realizing that she couldn't remember having smiled at all the past four days. "You'd better not be saying that just to humor me."

"Have I ever lied to you?" He sounded reproachful.

"No."

"And I never will. So will you go? Before you answer, remember that Jess is my boss and if I mess up this assignment he won't like it."

She chuckled softly. "That's blackmail, pure and simple."

"What's a little blackmail, if it means I can have my way with you?"

Warmth spread through her, though he had probably not meant anything sexual by it. He was most likely talking about getting her to accept the Stouts' invitation. But she was suddenly hot all over because his words had made her remember how easily he had had his way with her last Saturday night, how willing she had been to let him.

"Okay, already," she said, laughing to cover her loss of composure, "I'll go."

"Marty, have some more chicken." Jess Stout had made sure Marty's plate had plenty of food on it from the moment they sat down to dinner.

She smiled and shook her head. "I couldn't hold another bite, honestly, Jess." The Stouts had insisted that she call them by their first names.

"I hope you've saved room for dessert," Rose said. "It's hot apple cobbler." She was a short, white-haired woman with kind, blue eyes.

Marty exchanged a look with Walker and moaned. "I feel as though I'm being fattened for slaughter."

Everybody laughed before Jess grew serious and said, "We want you to feel at home, Marty. I know Walker told you I'm interested in hearing about your dreams, but don't feel you have to talk about it if you'd rather not. Truth is, I just wanted to meet the woman who's had this man wandering around like a sleepwalker the past week."

Walker groaned and Marty thought his face was actually a little flushed. "For God's sake, Jess, I worked three double shifts last week. The only sleep I got was walking around."

"So you say, Walker. So you say." Jess winked at Marty.

She smiled, suddenly feeling very happy. Walker wouldn't have had time to call her if he'd wanted to, since he was working double shifts. She looked at Walker and saw laughter in his eyes. He wanted to kiss her at that moment, and she knew they both felt it.

The evening had gone more smoothly than she'd expected, thanks to the Stouts. They were easy to be with; she felt she'd known them for a long time. It was rather a surprise, though, to discover that she no longer resented their curiosity about her precognition. "I don't mind talking about my dreams, Jess," she said. "What would you like to know?"

"Well—" He seemed startled. Evidently he hadn't expected her to be so willing to talk; Walker must have warned him she would be reticent. "I've read Walker's report, of course. I was just wondering if you'd remembered something more since the day you came to the station."

"No, I'm sorry. I've had the dream twice, and it was the same both times. I saw Julia Allman trying to get away from a man, but I didn't see the man's face. I'm not sure how much you know about ESP, but you simply can't force an experience. They come or they don't. People with ESP don't know how they do it. They don't even know if the interpretations they make are right or wrong. It's an unconscious process, you see. In fact, trying to force it practically guarantees failure. That's why psychics are often unsuccessful when they try to work with the police."

Rose was nodding her head. "It's just a feeling that comes from nowhere when you least expect it, and nobody can talk you out of it."

Marty turned to her. "That's exactly right. How did you know?"

"Because it happened to me. Only once, but I'll never forget it. It was almost twenty years ago. Our older son was spending the night with a friend. I'd gone to bed and about eleven, I came wide awake with the feeling that he was hurt. I just knew, that's all."

"I was still up, reading," Jess said. "She came into the living room and said we had to go and find Chris. I phoned the parents of the boy he was staying with, but the boys hadn't come in yet. Rose got dressed and insisted that we had to go and look for them."

"As we were leaving," Rose put in, "the phone rang. It was the hospital, calling to tell us that Chris and his friend had been in a car wreck. The other boy was hardly scratched, but Chris had several broken bones. It was months before he felt like himself again." She looked at Jess. "We laughed about it later, when we knew Chris would mend, and Jess said it must have been woman's intuition."

"From what you've told me, it sounds as though you had an episode of clairvoyance," Marty said.

"I've come around to that opinion myself," Jess said. "Back then, though, I don't believe we'd even heard the word."

Marty went on to tell them of some of her own experiences with precognition. The Stouts were such an interested, open-minded audience that she didn't wonder if they were thinking she was deluded. They took what she said at face value; she was sure of it.

Walker merely listened, his expression unreadable.

Soon the conversation returned to the missing coed. Rose said, "I keep thinking there's something we're overlooking—about Marty's dream."

"I've been over and over it in my mind," Marty said, "but I can't remember anything I haven't already told you."

"That kitchen you saw," Jess mused, "must be in an old house. The range wasn't built in and you didn't mention a dishwasher. Most houses built in the last twenty years have dishwashers."

"That's right," Marty agreed, "there wasn't a dishwasher."

Walker moved restlessly. "The majority of the houses in town were built more than twenty years ago. The newer houses are in the west-side additions. And we don't even know if the house is in Willow."

Rose nodded glumly. "Let's forget the dream then and concentrate on the kidnapped girls. What did they have in common?"

Jess patted his wife's shoulder. "Rose worries over police investigations as much as I do."

"Everybody in Willow had better be worried," Rose said. "It's a community problem. And, Jess, you have to admit that once or twice I've come up with an idea that was helpful to you."

Jess nodded. "You sure have, sugar."

Walker gazed at Marty, and she wondered what he was thinking. "About the only thing they seem to have in common is that they were both Willow State students."

"Are there physical likenesses?" Marty asked. "It's hard to tell from the newspaper pictures."

"They're about the same age, of course, and near the same size," Walker said. "And they're both brunettes." He pondered for a moment. "Come to think of it, I believe they both have brown eyes, too. But if you had seen them together, I'm not sure you would have been struck by their similarities."

"The man who took them might work at the college," Rose suggested.

"That was one of our first lines of investigation," Walker said, "and we're still pursuing it. Linda Niles disappeared at night from a café a few blocks off campus. But we believe Julia was taken from the campus sometime around noon. No one we've talked to remembers noticing anyone on campus that day who didn't belong there. The abductor could be a student or an employee of the college."

"On the other hand," Jess said, "he could have been passing through. Around noon there are a lot of people crossing the campus. Maybe he works nearby and was off for lunch."

"Or he could work at night," Walker put in. "He could have been on an evening meal break when he took Linda Niles. He could even be unemployed. But if he doesn't have a legitimate reason to be on campus, he evidently blends in well. Nobody we've talked to has mentioned any suspicious characters hanging around the college."

"Then he must either be a student or be young enough to be taken for one," Rose said.

"Which narrows it down to ten thousand young men, give or take a few," Jess muttered.

Rose sighed, "We aren't getting anywhere with this discussion, are we? Let's have dessert and talk about something more pleasant."

Marty followed Rose into the kitchen. "What can I do to help?"

"Get the bowls, on the second shelf there."

Marty set the bowls on the counter and Rose spooned warm cobbler into them. "I wanted to tell you how much I've enjoyed the evening," Marty said.

Rose touched Marty's hand. "We've enjoyed having you, dear. I hope we didn't put you on the spot with all that talk about your dreams."

"I didn't mind," said Marty truthfully. "I could tell that you and Jess don't have any rigid, preconceived opinions about ESP."

"When you've lived as long as we have," Rose said with a smile, "you're not as sure about anything as you once were. Besides, I've always felt in my heart that my own experience was more than a mother's anxiety. And woman's intuition—whatever that may be—didn't seem a strong enough term for it, either."

With an uncharacteristic impulsiveness, Marty hugged the older woman. Rose hugged her back and said, "Walker, you know, is a very methodical man. He's the only officer on the Willow police force with a college degree, and perhaps that was where he learned to be so organized in his thinking. In an investigation, he'll worry at loose ends like a bulldog until he fits everything into a pattern, however long it takes. But it isn't pigheadedness, Marty. He can admit it when he's wrong."

Marty picked up two of the dessert bowls. "Thank you for telling me that, Rose. I'm probably too defensive about my precognition, and too impatient with disbelievers."

They had dessert, followed by coffee in the living room. Nobody brought up ESP again, or the Allman case. Later, on the drive to Marty's house, Walker put his arm around her and pulled her next to him. Feeling relaxed and happy, she rested her head against his shoulder and perused his strong jawline through the screen of her lashes.

"I liked Jess and Rose very much," she murmured.

"It was mutual." He glanced around at her with a grin. "Jess wanted to know how in the world a beautiful woman like you had escaped matrimony till now. Jess thinks everybody should get married and live happily ever after, like him and Rose."

"What did you tell him?"

"I said I was sure it wasn't for lack of opportunity." He sobered. "You haven't ever been married, have you?"

"No. I was engaged once, but that was a long time ago."

"What happened?"

Why had she mentioned her engagement? The contentment she had been feeling the moment before receded a little. "He wasn't the man I thought he was," she said finally. "I'm just glad I found out before the wedding."

He pulled into her driveway, switched off the engine, and enveloped her in his arms. "I am, too," he said quietly. He bent his head to nuzzle her neck. "I don't like the thought of you belonging to another man, even before I knew you."

She snuggled up to him, smiling. "How can you be jealous of somebody you never even met? And, to set the record straight, a woman doesn't belong to a man, like his car or his TV set."

His laugh rumbled against her throat. "Oh, babe, you've got a lot to learn."

"I mean it." She tried to sound serious, but her mouth was twitching at the corners. "Don't be so possessive."

He lifted his head and grinned down at her. "It's born in a man, honey. You can't fight Mother Nature."

She couldn't argue with him when he was like this.

He kissed her lingeringly, then inquired, "Aren't you going to invite me in?"

She leaned back against his arms. "Would you like to come in, Walker?" she asked solemnly.

"I thought you'd never ask," he said and opened the driver's door, pulling her out of the car after him.

For some reason, this struck her as funny, and she giggled all the way across the front yard as she ran to keep up with his long strides. In the living room, she leaned against the wall, gasping, "I don't know why I'm laughing. The neighbors will think we're drunk."

He closed the front door and pulled her into his arms. "Ahh, Marty," he said softly, "I am drunk—on your charms."

"My, you do have a way with words, Officer Dietrick."

He kissed her, using his tongue to persuade her to part her lips. It took very little persuasion. She was turning to softness in his arms as he kissed her all over her face, on the tip of her nose, on her chin, at each corner of her mouth, and in her mouth again. The fierce excitement was filling her once more, demanding release. She wound her arms about his neck and slid her body erotically against his. She could feel the iron strength in his arms and hands and body, and she felt the tremor, too. The knowledge that she had such power over him made her blood pound with the rhythm of desire.

They hadn't turned on any lights and when, after long moments, he lifted his head and looked down at her, moonlight falling through the windows touched his craggy face with silver. For an instant she felt as though they were a part of something too grand to be flesh and blood. This can't be real, she thought wonderingly. With a shaky breath, she murmured, "Have you bewitched me, Walker Dietrick?"

In answer he pushed her jacket off her shoulders and down her arms. He then kissed her throat and, unbuttoning her dress, kissed the smooth curve of her shoulder. "Marty," he whispered hoarsely, desperately, "don't send me away." His mouth traveled across her skin, caressing and igniting.

Her breath escaped in a moan, and she took his hand. "Follow me." She led him through rooms that gilding moonlight had transformed into places of fantasy. She led him to her bed.

There were no words as they stood facing each other to undress. Her breathing was quick and shallow, and she could hear his ragged gasps as though he were unable to get the oxygen he needed. Then they were naked, standing in a pool of moonlight. His dark gaze swept over her, electrifying every corner of her mind. She took his hand and, bracing one knee on the bed, pulled him down to lie beside her.

He bent over her, and she stroked the taut muscles of his shoulders and back and felt him quiver with need. "You're trembling," she whispered, smiling up at him in sensuous understanding of what he was feeling, for she was trembling, too.

"You do that to me." His arms tightened convulsively around her and she pressed her flesh against his as a womanly confidence flooded through her.

He lifted her against his hard arousal and his mouth covered hers, pleading and demanding at once. She shifted to cradle him between her hips, all her senses overwhelmed, as though she were drowning. She ran her fingers through his hair and cradled his head in her hands.

"Walker," she whispered, her voice husky with passion. "Walker, love me." She moved against him with a need she could not control.

"Marty," he muttered against her lips. "You are mine. You belong to me. Do you understand?"

"Please," she cried softly. "Please, Walker..."

He kissed her arched throat and swollen breasts, and the pleasure was almost more than she could bear. But still it wasn't enough, not nearly enough....

Restlessly, her hands sought him, curling desperately, clinging. His moan of pleasure shook them both. Then he lifted himself and, holding her dazed eyes with a gaze so intense it was like a licking flame, he slid deep inside her.

Neither of them had any control over their bodies now. All they could do was ride the fierce, plunging waves together, clinging to each other as if to let go would be to fly off into space.

The wild climb began and rose rackingly and exploded suddenly. They cried out together as their bodies were rocked with ecstasy. He surged against her, shuddering. She closed her eyes and lifted a trembling hand to cradle his head against her breast.

Chapter 7

When she awoke the next morning, Marty found the coffee made and a note, in Walker's forceful scrawl, tacked to the kitchen message board.

I feel as though anything is possible this morning. I had to go to the station. It was too early to wake you. (I was tempted, though.) Don't forget, you're my woman, Marty Newland. Love,
Walker

She smiled softly as she read the words. *Anything is possible* . . . that could mean a great deal or very little. Last night's lovemaking had been marvelous, but that didn't mean the world was a different place this morning, or that she and Walker were different.

You're my woman...classic machismo, that. But she didn't mind. In fact, she rather liked it.

You're as dippy as Fern Small, Marty chided herself as she got ready to go to the clinic. The unflattering comparison did not seem to arouse much concern in her. Nor did it worry her excessively that she'd slept late and could not possibly make it in time for the eight o'clock meeting she had scheduled with Jerry and the clinic's accountant. Last night had left her as complacent as a well-fed cat.

She breezed into Jerry's office at eight-thirty. "Sorry I'm late, gentlemen. My alarm didn't go off this morning." Which was true enough; she hadn't set it.

Jerry was thoroughly irritated. She could tell by the thrust of his cleft chin. Also, by the way he bypassed civilities and got right to the heart of the matter. "You could have picked a better time to sleep in. Jim and I have been going over the budget for next year." He shuffled through the papers on his desk, snatched one and poked it at her. "Here's your copy. Now, where were we, Jim? Oh, yes, estimated grant income . . ."

Marty slid into a chair, sternly disciplining herself to keep from laughing at Jerry, a shockingly inappropriate reaction on her part. The budget was a serious matter, and the accountant had rearranged some appointments to fit them in today. Moreover, the budget would be presented to the clinic's governing board tomorrow, and she must be prepared to answer questions concerning it.

But what were budgets compared to a pair of teasing hazel eyes and a shock of dark-red hair? She had really lost it this morning; Walker had cast a spell on her last night. She shook her head in an effort to dislodge romantic foolishness. She ran her fingernail down the lines of figures until she found the one Jerry and the accountant were now discussing. Resolutely she pushed everything but the budget from her mind and entered the discussion. Jerry might even have forgiven her the late arrival if Dotty hadn't interrupted them a few minutes later.

"Marty, this just came for you." Dotty walked into the office and handed Marty a small, gift-wrapped box. Becoming aware of the dead silence that had greeted her entrance, Dotty quickly backed out again. "I thought it might be important," she said lamely and shut the door.

There was a gold foil sticker from Randall's, Willow's most stylish lady's shop, on the package. For the moment forgetting her two impatient male companions, Marty tore into the box and lifted out a gray, cashmere scarf. It was incredibly soft, perfectly beautiful, and very expensive she was sure. The small card inside, written in the same bold hand as the note tacked beside her kitchen phone, read: "This reminded me of your eyes." Smiling, she lifted the scarf to her cheek.

"Nice scarf. Who's it from?"

Marty's head jerked up at the terse sound of the accountant's voice. She replaced the scarf in the box hurriedly. "It isn't signed." She slid an apologetic look in Jerry's direction.

"Can we get on with the budget?" Jerry snapped.

"Yes, of course."

"Unless you and Dotty would like to throw a tea party in here."

Marty tried a small, joshing smile. "The budget, Jer."

"Are you quite sure you don't mind?" Jerry continued. Evidently further venting of his spleen was necessary. "We wouldn't want to bore you. Perish the thought...."

Marty glared at him, then addressed the accountant. "Would you mind explaining the item on line ten, please."

The meeting was concluded without further interruption. When the accountant had left them, Marty attempted to mend her fences. "Jerry, I'm really sorry about being so late. I'll go over the budget tonight. I'll be fully prepared to discuss it with the board tomorrow."

Jerry made a conciliatory gesture with his hands. "I'm sorry, too. I shouldn't have snapped at you. It's just not like you to be late for a meeting."

"I know. It won't happen again."

Jerry studied her from behind his desk. "Who's the scarf from?"

"The card wasn't signed..."

"I heard that. But you know who sent it, don't you?"

She smiled mysteriously. "I have a pretty good idea."

Jerry shook his head. "If I didn't know you so well, I'd think you were in love."

When she didn't respond, Jerry laughed and said, "Well, everybody's entitled to make a fool of himself at least once in his life."

Walker was having his own problems this morning. Shortly after he entered his office, he had a telephone call from Stan Rudley, the manager of Willow Nursing Home. "I hate to ask," Rudley said, "but could you possibly come out here and talk to Professor Vance? He was demanding to see you all day yesterday. I thought if we ignored him, he'd forget about it. This morning he tore his telephone from the wall and is threatening to throw his clothes into the hall if he isn't allowed to speak to you. He's been tranquilized, but it doesn't seem to have helped much."

"I think I can make it in about an hour," Walker said. Poor old Toliver. Still had the same bee in his bonnet, probably. He'd been wrong in assuming Tol would forget their earlier conversation. The professor had the memory of an elephant when it suited him. Walker really didn't have time to go all the way out to the nursing home, but he remembered Tol of the sharp mind and dry wit, from the days when Walker had been a student at Willow State. The professor had deteriorated rapidly in the years since then, but knowing what he had been, Walker couldn't refuse his request.

"Thanks, Walker. I'll go right now and tell him you're coming."

When Walker got to the home, Toliver was waiting for him in the living room. Several other residents occupied the room, reading or watching the television set, which was blaring loudly. The unmistakable antiseptic nursing-home aroma assailed Walker.

"Come back to my room," Toliver said as soon as Walker stepped inside. He marched stiffly ahead of Walker down the tiled hall, still very spry in spite of his advanced age. When they reached his room, he closed the door and turned accusing eyes on Walker. "You certainly took your time getting here." The electric ceiling light reflected off the professor's bald head.

"I wasn't told you wanted to see me until this morning," Walker said.

"Humph." Toliver walked over to the dresser and turned on his radio. Motioning Walker to the other side of the room, he hissed, "We'll have to talk with the radio on. This place is bugged."

"I thought you'd checked this room out thoroughly," Walker said.

"They got in after that somehow."

Walker wondered who "they" were. He knew it was useless to contradict him. He spoke into Toliver's ear. "I guess you want to know what I found out about the janitor."

Toliver nodded sagely.

"He's clean, Professor. Rudley swears he was working in the yard when the second coed disappeared. Rudley had him in sight all the time."

Toliver seemed to be in deep thought for a moment. Then he squinted at Walker. "They could be in it together, you know."

"No chance, Professor. Take my word for it."

Toliver pondered for another moment. "Then why won't Rudley let me have a telephone in here?"

Walker said judiciously, "Rudley says your phone was damaged."

Toliver snorted. "I told him the thing was bugged, but he wouldn't do anything. So I took care of it."

Walker nodded. "I'm sure Rudley will get the phone company out here in a day or two to put another one in for you."

Toliver's dark eyes snapped. "Please inform Mr. Rudley that if I don't have a telephone within twenty-four hours, I shall file a formal complaint against him."

"I'll do it," Walker agreed solemnly. "Now is there anything else I can do for you before I go, Professor?"

"Yes," said Toliver, "you can debug this room."

Walker thought about all the important police work awaiting him, and his patience almost snapped. But then he thought, since he was there, maybe he could mollify the old man. "Okay. You wait for me out in the hall." When Toliver left, Walker closed the door and turned off the radio. He moved a chair and the nightstand, in case Toliver was listening. Then he sat on the side of the bed, tapping his foot, and watched the second hand sweep the face of his watch. Five minutes later, he left the room. He found Toliver in the living room and, taking him aside, said confidentially, "All clear now, Professor."

Toliver eyed him narrowly. "I'm still giving the case top priority, Walker. If I come up with any new clues, I'll let you know."

Walker shook the professor's hand and left. Maybe he'll at least forget about the bugs now, Walker told himself as he drove back to the station. For an instant in there, he'd had a sneaking feeling the professor was putting him on. Was the old coot playing some kind of game with him out of sheer boredom? He couldn't much blame the old man if he was. Everybody needed some excitement in his life. It gave him something to tell Marty, and would make her laugh. He liked to hear her laugh. He liked everything about her, come to think of it. Just remembering last night made his temperature go up.

"Hell," he muttered. He had to get his mind on business. He had a murderer to find. And he had to get to Julia Allman before the maniac killed again—if Marty was right and Julia was still alive. He still wasn't sure how he felt about Marty's dream. But until they found a body, he had to assume the girl could still be saved.

Marty no longer thought seriously about not seeing Walker again. He had become too important to her happiness. Unwilling to put a stop to the affair, she compensated by telling herself that a woman could have a physical relationship with a man and keep her heart out of it, as easily as a man could.

After all, that was what Walker was doing, wasn't it?

She didn't dare let herself believe that Walker was in love with her. Even though he made her feel very special and cherished when they were together, he had never said that he loved her.

In rare objective moments, she realized that she was playing mental games with herself, the kind she tried

to help her clients see and overcome. Mostly such
moments came during her sessions with Fern Small. "I
know what I ought to do about Charley," Fern said in
one session. "I ought to tell him to get lost. Last week,
I almost did it. But then he looked at me with that
sweet smile of his, and I just couldn't. What it boils
down to, Miss Newland, is I love the man. I know he
doesn't treat me like he should, but I still love him. He
makes me unhappy sometimes, but other times he
makes me feel like a queen. I guess everything's a
trade-off. You understand what I'm trying to say?"

Marty understood perfectly. Who was she kidding,
thinking she could continue her affair with Walker and
keep her heart safely locked away? Was she really that
stupid? The truth was she was in love with Walker. She
wasn't going to lie to herself anymore, but she was
determined to keep it from Walker. All at once she remembered Dotty's warning about all the women
Walker had courted. None of them had lasted very
long, Dotty had said. Why had those relationships
ended? Was it because the women had begun to take
things too seriously? The thought terrified her. She
must be careful not to make that mistake and would
play it light and easy—on the surface, anyway.

By unspoken consent, she and Walker did not talk
about her dreams. He hadn't mentioned again their
"working together" on the case. Marty realized now
that the first time he had taken her out to talk about
ESP in connection with the Allman case, it had merely
been an excuse to be with her. Now that they were together frequently, he didn't need the excuse anymore.

It concerned her that Walker still did not believe she had precognition, but most of the time she could push the concern to the back of her mind.

Walker worked until five the next Sunday morning, went home to shower and sleep for a while, but arrived at Marty's house at the appointed time, noon, for brunch.

When he took her in his arms, she leaned back to get a good look at him. "You couldn't have slept long. You look beat."

He nuzzled her neck. "I'll sleep later. I needed to be with you." He took her earlobe between his teeth and nibbled, making her shiver. "I think I'm addicted. I have to have a dose of you at least every forty-eight hours or I start having withdrawal pain."

"Poor man." She laughed softly, the sound muffled against his shoulder, and leaned against him. He made her feel so womanly and so needed. She turned her head to bury her face in the dark, warm crook made by his neck and shoulder. He smelled wonderfully of soap and masculine cologne.

He took a deep breath and continued to hold her, his hand coming up to bury itself in her hair. "You feel so good in my arms."

"Mmm," she murmured happily, "I could stay here forever, but your omelet will burn."

He let her go reluctantly and sat down at the table, admiring the graceful sway of her lush little bottom in powder-blue corduroy jeans as she moved about the kitchen. Then he noticed the way her navy silk shirt hugged her pertly thrusting breasts and was tempted

to grab her and haul her off to bed immediately, omelet be damned. He reached for the cup of coffee she set
in front of him and brought it to his mouth. The hot
liquid burned all the way down, but it helped divert his
mind from the ache throbbing in him. Not from
Marty, though. He continued to watch her over the
rim of his mug. Her face had never been far from his
mind the past two weeks—a lovely face with a sweet,
generous mouth and large gray eyes that softened
when he smiled at her. How many women had he
known? He'd lost count. Yet since he met Marty he
hadn't had a spare thought for any of them. He would
have been hard put even to remember what they
looked like. Marty had beguiled and utterly bewitched him.

He didn't know what to do about it because he
wasn't sure what he wanted to do about it.

When Marty joined him at the table, she asked,
"Anything new in the Allman case?"

He shook his head. "You'll be glad to know we've
called off the surveillance of Grimes. There's just
nothing to connect him to Julia's disappearance, and
the overtime was playing havoc with the budget."

"You do think she's still alive, don't you?"

He hesitated, then said, "The fact that we haven't
found her body is a good sign. Also, the interval between the disappearance of Linda Niles and Julia's
kidnapping was two weeks, but it's been more than
two weeks since then and there hasn't been a third
kidnapping. There's no way of knowing if that's sig-
nificant, but it could mean the kidnapper is still holding Julia, alive."

His words jolted Marty. More than two weeks since Julia's disappearance? She hadn't realized so much time had passed, perhaps she hadn't wanted to realize it. She'd been absorbed in her own life and her relationship with Walker. She did a mental calculation and came up with the day's date, November twelfth, and her heart dropped. Julia's time was quickly running out.

Walker changed the subject, and she let herself be diverted. What could be gained by making herself sick, worrying?

Much later, after Walker had made slow, dreamy love to her and then fallen asleep beside her, she raised herself on one elbow and gazed through the bedroom window at the sleepy Sunday afternoon street. It was one of those rare, windless days that could set your teeth on edge if you lived daily with wind. It made you feel as though something ominous could happen any minute.

Marty shifted restlessly, trying not to wake Walker. She couldn't stop thinking about Julia. After the brief exchange over brunch, she hadn't brought up the subject with him again. She knew he needed a few hours' rest from the frustration of the case. Besides, rehashing accomplished nothing.

Inside Marty, the need to act on her fears was growing, becoming an unbearably heavy weight next to her heart. She knew better than to mention it to Walker. He would throw a fit if he thought she wanted to get personally involved in the investigation. After her failure in the matter of the hair clasp, she suspected he'd lost whatever faith in her extrasensory ability he'd had. The only thing that would impress

Walker now was physical evidence. So whatever she did for Julia, she would have to do it on her own.

Sighing, she lay back down and snuggled up to Walker's warm back. What was it Rose had said at dinner last week? *I keep thinking there's something we're forgetting—about Marty's dream.* Had they forgotten something? She replayed the dream again in her mind. Behind her closed eyelids, she saw Julia run into the kitchen, and then she saw the man—the dark hair, the thick neck, the broad muscular shoulders and arms.... He had to work out with weights regularly. It was the only way he could have developed those bulging muscles.

Suddenly she knew what they had overlooked. A man who worked out regularly had to do it somewhere. A health club? A small tingle of excitement ran through Marty. There couldn't be many health clubs in Willow. Someone stationed outside for a few evenings would probably get a look at most of the regular customers.

She wouldn't mention her idea to Walker yet, though, not until she had something more concrete to offer.

Quietly she got out of bed, leaving Walker napping, dressed stealthily, and went to find the phone book. Only two businesses were listed in the yellow pages under "Health Clubs," along with the YMCA.

She took down the addresses on a scrap of paper and tucked it in her purse. Walker would be working evenings this week. It was a perfect opportunity to set up a surveillance of her own.

You know the thrill of
escaping to a world of
Love and Romance as it
is experienced by
real men and real women..

Escape again...with 4 FREE novels and

**get more great Silhouette Intimate Moments® novels
—for a 15-day FREE examination—
delivered to your door every month!**

Silhouette Intimate Moments offers you romance for women...not girls. It has been created especially for the woman who wants a more intense, passionate reading experience. Every book in this exciting series promises you romantic fantasy...dynamic, contemporary characters...involving stories...intense sensuality...and stirring passion.

Silhouette Intimate Moments may not be for everyone, but if you're the kind of woman who wants more romance in her life, they will take you to a world of *real* passion, *total* involvement, and *complete* fulfillment. Now, every month you can thrill to the kind of romance that will take your breath away.

FREE BOOKS

Start today by taking advantage of this special offer—4 new Silhouette Intimate Moments romances (a $10.00 Value) *absolutely FREE,* along with a Cameo Tote Bag. Just fill out and mail the attached postage paid order card.

AT-HOME PREVIEWS, FREE DELIVERY

After you receive your 4 free books and Tote Bag, every month you'll have the chance to preview 4 more Silhouette Intimate Moments novels —*as soon as they are published!* When you decide to keep them, you'll pay just $9.00, (a $10.00 Value), *with never an additional charge of any kind and with no risk!* You can cancel your subscription at any time simply by dropping us a note. In any case, the first 4 books, and Tote Bag are yours to keep.

EXTRA BONUS

When you take advantage of this offer, we'll also send you the Silhouette Books Newsletter free with each shipment. Every informative issue features news on upcoming titles, interviews with your favorite authors, and even their favorite recipes.

Get a Free
Tote Bag, too!

**VERY BOOK YOU RECEIVE WILL BE
BRAND-NEW FULL-LENGTH NOVEL!**

CLIP AND MAIL THIS POSTPAID CARD TODAY!

NO POSTAGE
NECESSARY
IF MAILED
IN THE
UNITED STATES

BUSINESS REPLY CARD

FIRST CLASS   PERMIT NO. 194   CLIFTON, N.J.

Postage will be paid by addressee

**Silhouette Books
120 Brighton Road
P.O. Box 5084
Clifton, NJ 07015-9956**

Escape with 4 Silhouette Intimate Moments novels (a $10.00 Value) and get a FREE Tote Bag, too!

Silhouette Intimate Moments®

Silhouette Books, 120 Brighton Rd., P.O. Box 5084, Clifton, NJ 07015-9956

Yes, please send me the FREE and without obligation, 4 new Silhouette Intimate Moments novels along with my Cameo Tote Bag. Unless you hear from me after I receive my 4 FREE books, please send me 4 new Silhouette Intimate Moments novels for a free 15-day examination each month as soon as they are published. I understand that you will bill me a total of just $9.00 (a $10.00 Value) with no additional charges of any kind. There is no minimum number of books that I must buy, and I can cancel at any time. The first 4 books and Cameo Tote Bag are mine to keep, even if I never take a single additional book.

NAME _____

(please print)

ADDRESS _____

CITY _____ STATE _____ ZIP _____

Terms and prices subject to change. Your enrollment is subject to acceptance by Silhouette Books.
SILHOUETTE INTIMATE MOMENTS is a registered trademark.

CT8865

During the next few days, Marty learned how boring a stake-out could be. She had, she decided, never fully appreciated policemen, particularly detectives, before. Monday evening, she parked outside the YMCA for three hours. A cold front had swept down on southwestern Oklahoma Monday morning and was evidently going to hang around for a while. Sitting in her car outside the Y, Marty nearly froze to death, even though she started the engine and ran the heater for a bit every fifteen minutes.

Tuesday evening, she dressed more warmly and took a blanket and a thermos of coffee with her when she went to the Body Works on Main Street. After three more fruitless hours, she drove home, disappointed, her nerves jangling from too much caffeine. She hadn't seen anyone entering or leaving either the Y or the Body Works who reminded her of the man in her dream. But she hadn't been very close and the men had been wearing coats or jackets, and hurrying. This wasn't getting her anywhere, she realized.

She decided on a different approach for Wednesday evening. Since the Willow Physical Performance Center catered to both sexes, she went inside and asked to have the program explained to her. The manager was a short, heavy-set man in his forties whose stomach bulge hid his belt buckle. He obviously didn't avail himself of the center's facilities, and he didn't seem too happy about leaving his chair and portable television set behind the front desk to show Marty around.

"Over here are the treadmills," he grumbled, leading the way. Marty followed at his heels, asking a question now and then and trying to appear interested in what he was saying, while at the same time scanning the men on the floor, looking for a dark head above a thick neck and broad shoulders.

"How often do most of your members work out?" she inquired.

"Three or four times a week usually," her guide said. "A few come every day—the ones who are really into it."

If the man she was looking for worked out only three times a week, Marty thought, she might also miss him indefinitely, switching from club to club every evening as she had been doing. If he came during the day, she was wasting her time altogether. "Do you have many people here in the middle of the day?" she asked.

"Not as many as at night, but there's always somebody around."

A bulging biceps caught Marty's eye. Somebody was lifting weights just around the corner, but she could only see one arm and shoulder. Backing away from her guide, she craned to get a look at the man.

"Lady, do you wanta see the graded exercise room or doncha?"

She glanced back and saw her guide waddling away from her toward a door that led to another part of the club. She took two more backward steps and the weight lifter finally came into her line of vision. He was big and muscled, all right, but blond. She ran to catch up with her disgruntled guide.

A few minutes later, the manager told her to look around as long as she wanted and he'd be at the front desk if she had any more questions. Marty wandered around, pretending an interest in the weight machines, until people began to cast puzzled glances her way. Thoroughly discouraged, she decided she'd probably seen everyone in the club by now, anyway.

Just as she approached the front desk, she saw a dark-haired, broad-shouldered man leaving. He must have been in the dressing room while she was looking around. He was putting on a quilted down jacket and paused just inside the front door. He set his gym bag down, zipped up the jacket, drew gloves from his pockets and put them on. Then he stooped, picked up the bag again, and pushed through the door.

For a moment, Marty stood, paralyzed. Suddenly a tremor raced through her. The man who had just left the club could be the man in her dream. If only she'd gotten a better look at him. She went to the desk. Her erstwhile guide sat in his chair, his hands behind his head, engrossed in a popular prime-time soap.

Marty cleared her throat loudly. "That man who just left looked like somebody I know. Can you tell me his name?"

He glanced over his shoulder at her. "I didn't see him."

"He's about this tall." Marty indicated with her hand. "Dark hair, big shoulders."

He squinted at her suspiciously. "Who'd you say he looked like?"

Marty blurted the first name that came into her head. "Jerry Macomber. I haven't seen him in ages."

Grunting, he got up and looked at a sheet attached to a clipboard on the desk. "Nope, there's no Jerry Macomber here." He went back to his chair.

Marty hesitated. Evidently club members signed in and out. She edged closer to the clipboard, trying to read it upside down. The man she was interested in should have signed out at 7:45. But she couldn't read the sheet from where she stood. She stepped closer and laid her arm on the desk. Slowly she nudged the clipboard around so that it was right-side up. The sheet contained a list of names with arrival and departure times beside them. She ran her gaze down the sign-out column. There it was: 7:45.

"Anything else I can do for you, lady?" The manager was looking over his shoulder at her again. "Hey, what're you doing with that clipboard?" He started to get up.

Her gaze raced across the line to the name on the left. Bill Welch, it said. She looked up and smiled. "You've been very helpful. Thanks."

Trudging back to her car, she said the name over and over in her mind. Bill Welch. An ordinary name. She was tempted to go into the café down the street and look up the name in the phone book. There might be several Welches in town, but, if luck was with her, there would be only one Bill.

However, Walker had switched shifts with another officer that day and was due at her house at eight o'clock. She would have to wait until later to search for Bill Welch.

Strangely she felt relieved, as though she'd been given a reprieve.

Chapter 8

"Hey, anybody home?" Walker leaned across the
coffee table that separated them and snapped his fingers. They had been playing Trivial Pursuit for a half
hour, and he was winning by a mile. Not because he
was so much better at trivia questions, but because
tonight Marty's mind was elsewhere. She had been
distracted ever since he got there. They had, in fact,
arrived at her house simultaneously. He'd pulled up
his car behind hers in the drive and followed her inside. When he asked where she'd been, she'd said
something vague about running errands. But she
hadn't had any packages, and he'd had the feeling she
was hiding something.

She blinked at him now and asked, "What was the
question?"

He propped his elbow on his jeaned knee and slid his gaze down the card he was holding. They were sitting on the carpet, on either side of her oak coffee table. "What card game," he read for the second time, "has variations called Canfield, Klondike and Spider?"

She had removed her shoes and now examined her white-socked feet as though she might find the answer written there. She wiggled her toes and looked up at him. "That's the silliest thing I ever heard. What has it got to do with sports, anyway?"

"The category is sports and leisure, my lovely. So answer the question."

"Poker."

"Wrong. It's Solitaire." He bent over and planted a kiss on her nose, then threw the die. He moved his marker to a yellow space and looked at her expectantly. He'd lost her again. She was staring out the darkened window, separated from him by her thoughts. Had she been any other woman of his acquaintance, he'd have found an excuse to leave. But she wasn't any other woman....

Where had she been just before he arrived tonight? Wherever it was, she obviously didn't want to talk about it. This wasn't the first time during the past few days that he'd sensed she had shut a part of herself off from him. He didn't like the way it made him feel. In fact, it scared the hell out of him.

It had occurred to him that she might be seeing another man. He even had an idea about who it might be—Jerry Macomber. Walker had met Marty's colleague at the clinic recently when he'd gone there to pick up Marty for lunch. She had been on the telephone, so he'd talked to Macomber for a few minutes. He seemed a nice enough guy, and he was good-looking. Walker knew that Macomber had tried to date Marty in the past. He'd found that out by questioning Dotty, but Dotty had said she didn't think Marty was interested. Walker wanted to believe that, but the last few days he'd found himself imagining Marty and Macomber together.

The role of the jealous suitor was a new one for Walker, and it bewildered him. Before Marty, he would have said he didn't have a jealous bone in his body. It had never bothered him if a woman he'd been seeing went out with another man. There were no strings in those relationships; he hadn't wanted any. But now, when he thought about Marty seeing any other man, he actually wanted to punch the guy.

"Oh, I'm sorry, Walker. You landed on yellow?" Marty pulled a card from the box next to her and read, "Who discovered Jamaica?"

Walker wrenched his mind away from a tormenting picture of Marty kissing Jerry Macomber. "Christopher Columbus."

She cocked her head. "Did you see the answer?"

His eyes narrowed in mock indignation. "Are you suggesting that I cheat?"

"Well, no—only, how did you know that?"

"Brilliant powers of deduction." He tapped a finger against his temple. "Besides," he added with a grin, "Columbus was the only discoverer I could think of." He added a yellow pie to his marker, filling the last empty space.

Marty looked at her own marker, which had only two of the pie-shaped spaces filled, and shook her head. "Let's quit. I concede defeat."

Walker began to put the game pieces back in their box. "Might as well. Your mind isn't on the game, anyway." It was a not-very-subtle hint for her to tell him what was on her mind, but she didn't take it.

"I'll make us some hot chocolate."

Walker found her in the kitchen a few minutes later. There was no evidence of preparations for hot chocolate. She was leaning against the sink, seemingly examining the leaves on a sick-looking ivy plant on the window ledge. But Walker would have bet her mind wasn't on the plant. When he touched her, she jumped.

"Oh, Walker, you scared the wits out of me!"

He caught her in his arms. "I'm sorry, honey, I thought you heard me come into the room."

"No," she murmured and let her head drop against his shoulder.

Without her shoes on, she seemed even smaller and more fragile than usual. To hell with subtlety. He'd just come right out with it. "Marty, something's bothering you. What is it?"

"Nothing," she said, feeling safe and warm in his embrace.

"Don't hide things from me, please."

After a long moment, she sighed, "It's just business. Somebody I'm counseling."

His arms tightened around her. "Are you sure that's all it is?"

"Well..." she countered, "I was wondering why you've been here two hours and you haven't made a serious pass yet."

"Oh, Marty," he breathed, and she felt relieved laughter shake his frame. Combing his hands into her shining hair he drew her head back, and he looked into her eyes. "I've been restraining myself. I don't want you ever to feel that all I want from you is to get you into bed. I enjoy just being with you."

She kissed the pulse that was beating at the base of his throat. "But you wouldn't mind getting me in bed, would you?"

"No—" Walker swallowed. "I wouldn't mind."

She laughed a breathless laugh. "Good, because I've decided I'm going to seduce you." Gently she lifted her hand to stroke his cheek. "Are you going to make it very difficult for me?"

He bent and kissed her. "I don't think I have the self-control to make it difficult. In fact, this is going to be the easiest seduction you ever heard of...." His mouth covered hers with a desperate urgency that made her melt against him. "Do whatever you want to me, honey," he whispered against her lips. "I need you so much."

"Whatever I want?" She gave a low, throaty chuckle. "My goodness, where shall I start?"

In her bedroom, he exerted all the self-control he possessed to remain impassive while she undressed him with slow exactitude, as though she had embarked upon a solemn ritual.

"Umm, I love to feel your skin." She ran her hand slowly across his back as she divested him of his undershirt, then down his lean, hair-roughened flank. He sucked in a loud breath as she discarded the last item of clothing, his briefs. "Walker, you're magnificent," she said softly.

"For you," he breathed, "I can be anything." Remaining impassive any longer was impossible. With hands that held a tremor, he undressed her. Then he put his hands at her waist and lifted her to sit on the bed. He bent to remove her socks, and kissed her instep.

She caught her breath as though the kiss had burned her. He was suddenly on fire, and he stripped off her lacy panties.

Then his mouth was on hers, his hand covering her breast, and his body fitted itself to hers as he pressed her down into the softness of the bed.

He felt the loss of himself that he had never felt with any other woman, the slow sensation and feminine aroma of her, the plunge into the reeling darkness as his body became one with hers, the incredible exaltation, and then the paroxysms that racked him to his depths . . . the little death. . . .

He awoke to the distant drumming of rain on the roof, aware of an uneasiness just below the level of consciousness. He turned his head on the pillow. The beautiful, sleeping face beside him was that of an angel . . . and there was something of the stranger in it, too.

He lay quietly, listening to the rain, and thought back over the evening. Then he knew what was making him uneasy. After being deeply absorbed in her own thoughts all evening, Marty had instigated love-making when he tried to find out what was troubling her. As much as he wanted to deny it, he knew she'd had an ulterior motive. Marty—his Marty—practicing feminine wiles on him to divert his attention. Because she didn't want to tell him what was bothering her. She was keeping something from him. She had been soft and willing in his arms tonight as she whispered sweet, erotic messages in his ear; but that part of her that she had shut off from him was as safely locked away as before.

What was she hiding?

Another man?

God, the mere thought made his chest feel as though somebody had rammed a poker through it. He could ask her, point-blank and didn't think she would actually lie to him. But did he really want to hear what she had to say?

Damn, he wanted all her free time and attention. He couldn't stand the idea that she ever thought of any other man but him. He was gettting positively paranoid on the subject, acting like a . . . a man in love.

The idea burst upon him like a comet, illuminating the darkest corners of his mind.

Love. It had happened to him, at last. He'd fallen like a ton of bricks, just as Jess had always predicted he would. He was staggered by the knowledge, which must have been somewhere in the back of his mind for days.

He wondered how she would react if he told her? Well, he wouldn't know that for a while. He didn't think Marty was ready to hear it, and he wasn't confident enough to risk telling her. Not yet.

It was well past midnight, but he knew he wasn't going to sleep again for a while. Although he had once stayed with Marty until morning, he could sense that she didn't want him to make a habit of it. He suspected it would represent too much of a commitment for her. More evidence, if he needed any, that she wasn't ready to hear any talk of love.

He would go down to the station and see what was going on there. If he went home, he would only prowl his house and brood over the revelations of this night. Fighting down an impulse to wake Marty and make love to her again, to brand her once more as his own, he slipped from the bed and got dressed in the darkness.

Marty stirred and murmured sleepily, "Walker..."

He bent over the bed, tucked the covers around her lovingly and brushed a kiss across her mouth. "I have to leave, honey. Go back to sleep. I'll turn out the lights and lock the door."

Marty waited until she heard the sound of Walker's car leaving before she got up. The wind-driven rain was blowing hard enough to make the bungalow's windows rattle. Sharp enough to cut you off at the pockets, as Dotty was wont to say.

Marty went into the kitchen and made the hot chocolate she had meant to fix before. Earlier that evening she'd tried to look up Welch in the phone book. She hadn't found the name, though, before she'd heard Walker coming. She'd put the phone book away hurriedly and gone to the window to examine the ivy plant she'd too often forgotten to water. Walker had known she was preoccupied tonight; she wasn't very good at dissembling.

She got the phone book and sat down at the kitchen table with the steaming cup of chocolate. Six Welches were listed. There was no Bill, but she found a W. L. and a W. C. Either or both of the *W*s could stand for William. One of them lived at 25 Cherry Lane, the other on Thirty-fifth Street. Before she went to bed, Marty wrote down both addresses, then sat for some time sipping her chocolate and thinking about her next move.

After work the next day, she bought a hamburger and coffee at a fast food drive-in, then drove by 25 Cherry Lane. She parked at the end of the block, ate the hamburger, and took a paperback novel from her purse. She settled down for a long wait.

A few minutes later, a woman came out of the house she was parked in front of. Marty didn't see her coming and jumped when she tapped on the window. She gave the glowering woman what she hoped was a friendly smile and rolled down the window.

"Can I help you?" The woman had probably been watching Marty from the moment she parked. Lord, what if she'd called the police?

"I'm waiting for somebody."

"Why'd you park in front of my house?" The woman asked, belligerence in every syllable.

"Er, because I have a clear view of the Welch house from here. I'm an insurance agent." It sounded ex-

actly like the lie it was. Heaven help her, she wasn't
any good at this. The woman was staring at her suspiciously. She probably thinks, Marty decided, I'm
casing the neighborhood for a likely house to rob.
"Mr. Welch is on my prospect list," she added, smiling for all she was worth.

The woman snorted. "Lady, you're a little late.
Warren Welch died last year."

"Oh, dear, I'm so glad you told me. I can't believe
my list is so outdated."

"I can tell you right now, his widow can't afford to
buy any more insurance than what she already has."
She glowered at Marty. "You're all alike. Badgering
people in their homes. If we listened to you, we'd be
spending all our income on insurance."

Insurance had been a bad choice. The woman was
positively hostile on the subject. "Well, thank you
very much. I'd better move along to my next prospect." Marty rolled up the window and drove away.
The scowling woman watched the car until it was out
of sight. Marty wondered worriedly if the woman had
memorized her license plate number. For a moment,
she was tempted to go home and forget trying to find
Bill Welch. But the thought of Julia Allman's danger
kept her from giving up.

After some searching, she found the other house.
Thirty-fifth Street was on the south edge of Willow.
The modest houses sat on oversized lots, some seemed
to be as large as an acre. They had probably been sold
as acreages in the country before the town grew out to
meet them. The address she was looking for was the

last house on the street. It was separated from the nearest house by about a third of a block.

Marty watched the dark house for more than an hour, frustrated because she had no feeling about whether it was the house in her dream. The temperature was dropping, and even with the blanket tucked around her legs she felt chilled through. It was almost eight o'clock when she gave up and drove home.

Her phone was ringing when she let herself in. It was Walker. "I've been calling you since six o'clock."

She didn't know whether to be irritated or pleased that he was keeping such close tabs on her. "I went out for a hamburger."

"It takes two hours to eat a hamburger?"

Irritation won out over pleasure. "Would you like me to keep a log for you so you'll know where I am at all times?"

There was a long pause. "I'm sorry. I was worried, but that's no excuse for subjecting you to the third degree."

She was immediately contrite, too. "I shouldn't have snapped at you. After eating, I drove around for a while. Lately, this house seems lonely when I'm here by myself in the evening." It was the closest she had yet come to admitting how much she was beginning to depend on him. As soon as the words were out, she wished she hadn't said them. Walker had given her no reason to think she meant any more to him than the women he'd known before. She mustn't start confusing the truth with what she wanted to believe. She tried to rob her admission of its effect by saying, "Maybe I should get a pet."

She heard him take a deep breath. "I'll be glad when I'm working days again." As with many of Walker's statements, she couldn't be sure if he meant to imply anything personal by this one.

"So will I," she admitted quietly.

"Maybe I can switch shifts with Phillips, Saturday. We could go to a movie or something."

"That would be nice."

We sound more like casual friends than lovers, Marty thought. She wished that Walker was with her right now; when they made love she could almost forget her doubts and insecurity.

"I'll talk to him tomorrow. I have to go now. Lock up tight before you go to bed."

His concern for her safety made her feel warm all over. Silly idiot, she chided herself. "I will. Good night, Walker."

"'Night, honey."

Friday evening, Marty returned to the house on Thirty-fifth Street. This time there were some lights on inside. She parked about halfway between the house and its nearest neighbor. After a few minutes, it dawned on her that everybody who lived in the house was probably at home by now. She might not see anyone if she sat there all night, and she couldn't think of a legitimate-sounding excuse for going to the door. Besides, the idea scared her too much. She might as well go home. She reached for the ignition key, and suddenly the front door of the house opened and a man came out. Before he closed the door behind him, Marty saw him in the light from inside. He was carrying a small satchel, like a gym bag. Oh, Lord, it was Welch!

He walked toward the car parked in the driveway. When he reached it, he turned and looked up the street. Marty had to stifle an impulse to duck down out of sight. He seemed to be staring directly at her. Maybe he'd noticed her car before he came outside. She didn't know which would seem less suspicious—to stay put or drive away. She'd had a story all worked out, in case anybody questioned her, but suddenly she couldn't remember what it was. He just kept standing there beside his car, staring. He could probably see that there was somebody in her car.

She took a deep, calming breath when he got into his car and started the engine. Then she realized he would have to drive by her; it was a dead-end street. Marty huddled in the corner of the front seat where the shadows seemed thickest. Perhaps he hadn't seen her, after all. She hunched down, making herself as small as possible.

The car lights approached. Only another few seconds and she could get out of there. Then, horror of horrors, the car slowed as it came nearer, and finally stopped. Welch was leaning across the car seat, peering into Marty's car. Looking right at her!

Panic struck. Her hand shook so violently she could barely turn the ignition key. He was rolling his window down now! Marty's engine caught, and she depressed the accelerator. Thank goodness she'd had the foresight to reverse her car before she parked so that she faced the escape route. Her tires squalled loudly as she took off. At the corner, she slowed only enough to make the turn, then sped up again. Several blocks away, she chanced a look in her rearview mirror. No car lights were reflected there. He hadn't followed her.

But her heart wouldn't stop racing. She slowed slightly for the rest of the drive home. It was only when she got out of the car and the cold wind hit her that she realized she was drenched with sweat. She raced inside, then locked and bolted the door.

Without turning on a light, she sagged into the nearest chair. What if Welch had seen her at the health club and recognized her tonight? She willed herself to think calmly. He couldn't find out her name. She hadn't given it to the manager at the health club.

What if he knew her license plate number?

If he reported her, she would say she'd been looking for a friend's house. That, she remembered, was the story she had concocted before leaving home tonight. Dotty lived on Thirty-third Street, although not so far south. If anybody asked, Marty would say she'd been searching for Dotty's address. There was no way they could prove she was lying.

She had panicked unnecessarily. Did one ever get used to this sort of thing? she wondered. She was glad that it was Friday. Walker was trying to get tomorrow night off to take her to a movie, and they would probably spend Sunday together since it was his day off. She had the weekend to get over tonight's scare.

Unfortunately, she didn't have the weekend in which to gather her courage, after all. Walker called later that night to tell her he couldn't find anybody willing to change shifts with him. He had to work Saturday night. Marty hung up, almost overcome with disappointment. She had come within an inch of telling him about Welch and asking him to run a check on him. At the last minute she'd bitten back the words; Walker would only think she was off on another tangent.

Then her glance fell on the kitchen calendar. Tomorrow would be November eighteenth. She couldn't wait until Monday to go back to Welch's house. Somehow she had to get a look at that kitchen. If it was the kitchen in her dream, then she could go to Walker and he would have to listen to her.

When she got there Saturday evening, several lights were on in the Welch house, and the same car was parked in the drive. More cautious this time, she parked further away than she had the night before. She watched the house for an hour, but nobody arrived or left. She had several choices. She could give up and go home, but then she'd feel compelled to try again another night. She could go boldly to the front door and say she was looking for the house of her friend, give Dotty's address. But she probably wouldn't be able to see the kitchen from the front porch. Besides, she might as well face it, she didn't have the nerve to confront Bill Welch face to face at his front door. That left window-peeking—breaking the law. But how else was she going to get a look at the kitchen?

If she was going to do it, she'd have to do it right away, before she talked herself out of it. Heaven help her.

She got out of her car and looked up and down the street. Nobody was stirring. Please let all the dogs be inside with their masters, she prayed as she walked

stealthily away from her car. She angled across the
open field separating Welch's house from its neighbor. The kitchen was probably in the back.

It seemed to take forever to get to the corner of the
house, but she didn't dare walk faster for fear of
stumbling in the dark and being heard by somebody
inside the house. Eventually she reached the house and
stopped for a moment, listening. Nothing.

Light from two back windows made pale rectangles
on the dead grass of the yard. Picking her way carefully, Marty circled around the lighted areas, then slid
noiselessly into the strip of darkness between the house
and the rectangles of light. She might be able to see
into the house if she stretched to her full height. Bracing her hands against the house, she lifted herself on
tiptoe.

She heard a rustling behind her and her heart leaped
into her throat. She whirled around.

The stocky form of a man stepped out of the shadows. "What the hell do you think you're doing!"

Chapter 9

Marty was incapable of speaking. Up close, Bill Welch looked as big as a mountain. He also looked enraged. She simply couldn't think and was aware only of a monstrous panic. She did the only thing she was capable of; she ran.

Behind her, she heard him yelling. "Hey, come back here! What the..."

If he decided to chase her, he could probably catch her. Terror fueled her body and her legs pumped furiously. She expected every second to feel a heavy hand clamp down on her shoulder. But it didn't happen. She reached her car and wrenched the door open. Scrambling inside, she slammed the door and locked it.

She looked toward the Welch house and fumbled in her coat pocket for her keys. It was too dark to see much, but she thought there was a shadowy form the size of a man near the corner of the house. Welch was standing there, watching her. Suddenly the shadow detached itself from the larger shadow of the house and strode toward her with a sort of grim resolution.

She felt total panic again. She gripped the keys and held them near her face to separate the ignition key from the others. With her heart trying to leap from her chest, she managed to get the key into the ignition and turn it. The engine ground, caught and then died.

This simply could not be happening.

From the corner of her eye she saw Welch. He had reached the edge of the yard. He was less than fifty feet away now and still coming, relentlessly. Would he try to get into the car, break the window... ?

She twisted the key. The engine caught again and she rammed her foot down on the accelerator. The car leaped forward, the tires squealing.

The car jerked and coughed. She let up on the accelerator and it smoothed out. At the corner, she had to stop for a car passing on the intersecting street. Fearfully, she twisted to took through the rear window. Welch was standing at the curb where her car had been parked, looking after her.

The cross street was clear now. She wheeled around the corner as fast as she dared and roared to the stoplight two blocks north. Fortunately there wasn't much traffic. She sat at the stoplight, waiting for what seemed forever until it turned green. Her hands gripped the steering wheel, her breathing loud in the chill silence. At last the green light flashed on, and she sped across the intersection.

What if he followed her in his car? What would she do?

She jerked her thoughts back from the stark edge of fear. One thing at a time, she counseled herself. If Welch followed, she wouldn't stop at her house. She would go somewhere public and try to lose him there—the mall. Her mind was beginning to work again. She took a complicated, roundabout route home. When she was sure that Welch hadn't followed her, she turned onto Ash Street and drove to the bungalow.

Switching off the engine and the lights, she sat in the dark car for a few moments to make doubly certain she hadn't been followed. No other car passed in the street. She gripped the house key and got out of the car, easing the door closed behind her. Feeling terribly exposed, she raced to the house, unlocked the door, and practically fell inside.

She didn't turn on any lights for several minutes. There was enough illumination from the yard lamp for her to make her way through the rooms without stumbling into the furniture. She went through the house, closing all the draperies, before she allowed herself to switch on a light. Then she removed her coat and went to the kitchen to brew tea. The mundane task seemed to calm her. Welch had no way of knowing who she was or how to find her, she assured herself.

She hadn't seen his kitchen, but she couldn't risk going back there again. She had failed at the one thing that might have led her to Julia Allman and exposed herself to incredible danger in the attempt. She must have been out of her mind to think she could play detective. As her fear subsided, it left her with a feeling of being totally defeated.

She carried her tea into the living room and curled up on the couch. She drank the tea, set the cup aside and felt drained, beaten.

She was still sitting there, trying not to think about what was happening to Julia Allman, when she heard a car turn into her driveway. Galvanized, she jumped up and turned off the living room light. Could Welch have found her, after all?

She crept to the window and moved the drapery just enough to peer out through a narrow crack. It was a police car! Walker got out of it and walked toward the house. Had he gotten off duty early? Maybe he was on patrol and had only stopped for a few minutes. It didn't matter why he was here; he couldn't have come at a better time. The sight of him made her feel safe for the first time since she'd confronted Welch. She switched the light back on and ran to the door.

"Hi!"

She wanted him to take her in his arms, but he didn't. He walked right past her into the living room, almost as though he was angry. She shut the door and turned to face him. He was just standing there, with a strange look on his face. Formidable. That was the word that came to her mind to describe the look. His stance, feet spread, hands on his hips, his shoulders looking even broader than usual in the black leather jacket, was actually intimidating. If it were anybody but Walker...

"Where have you been tonight?" he demanded.

What was going on? Who did he think he was, *demanding*? She was starting to get mad. "We've been through this already," she retorted. "You don't own me, Walker. Where I've been this evening is none of your business."

Something flared in his hazel eyes. He *was* angry. Why had be picked tonight to be possessive? She didn't want to argue with him. All she wanted was to feel his arms around her.

"It's my business," he bit out, "when an outraged citizen comes to the station, claiming he caught you looking in his window."

She gaped at him. "That's impossible! How did he—" She broke off, flustered. Welch couldn't know who she was!

"He? You mean William Welch? Then you were there, at his house tonight." He ran his hand through his thick hair and looked away as though he didn't enjoy the sight of her right then. When his gaze came back to her, he looked even angrier than before. "Don't you know trespassing is against the law? As for window-peeking—" He threw his head up and grunted with disgust. "What in God's name were you doing there?" he barked furiously.

"How did he know my name?" she asked in a small voice.

"He took down your license plate number and called the station. Phillips took the call. I pulled rank to get the assignment of checking it out. I've just come from Welch's house. He is one mad guy, and I don't think I blame him." His words were hard and sharp, like bullets. "Answer my question, Marty. What were you doing there?'' His demeanor was all grim police officer questioning a suspect. How could she ever have thought he was gentle?

She stared at him for a long moment. Then her shoulders sagged and she went to the sofa and sat down, farther away from him. But he followed and stood over her, waiting.

"I—I thought I could find Julia Allman."

He didn't even look surprised. Of course, he must have suspected her reason for being at the Welch house. "You've decided Welch is the murderer? Why?" He sounded resigned, but not as though he believed she had any legitimate reason for suspecting Welch. Did he think she was running around town looking in *all* the windows?

"The man in my dream was very muscular. I told you that. I told you he must work out with weights." She waited for him to comment, but he didn't. She continued, driven to make him understand. "It occurred to me that he had to work out somewhere, a health club probably. Recently I've been parking outside the clubs in the evenings, watching the men who come and go. That's where I'd been the other night before you got here, the Physical Performance Center. I pretended to be interested in joining. The manager showed me around. I saw Welch leaving—he had dark hair, and he was muscular. He could have been the man in my dream. I found his name on the checkout sheet. There are only two W. Welches in the phone book. The other one died last year."

"Welch said he saw you last night, parked near his house. But he couldn't get your license number until tonight."

"I needed to see who lived there. When Welch came out of the house, I recognized him from the club. But I still couldn't be certain he was the right man. The only way I could think of to be sure was to go back and try to get a look at his kitchen. That's what I was doing when he caught me."

"Why didn't you tell me?"

"Would you have believed me? Would you have tried to help me?"

He sat down beside her. "You little fool." His face looked bleak. She realized that he was afraid for her, and then suddenly he was angry again. His hands came out and gripped her upper arms. "Don't you realize what you did was dangerous? If Welch had been the murderer, do you think he would have let you get away?" His grip was painful, but she didn't think he realized it.

"You're hurting me."

Abruptly, he pulled her against him, his arms closing around her convulsively. "My God, Marty, when I think of you out there alone...if you had been right..."

She closed her eyes. His closeness made her feel faint, as though she just that moment understood the danger she had put herself in. She could have died tonight. "When you were at his house, did you see the kitchen?"

"Yes. It's small, with natural pine cabinets and brown square tiles on the floor. The table is in a separate breakfast room. And Welch doesn't live there alone. He has a wife and two children."

Welch couldn't be the one, then, and she had more than half convinced herself that he was. She shivered and Walker's arms tightened around her even more. "I had to do something. Julia Allman has been gone more than two weeks. Her time is running out."

He gripped her shoulders and looked down into her face. "For all we know, she's already dead. She probably *is* dead. He killed the first girl within twenty-four hours of taking her. He's crazy, Marty. He's got some kind of hang-up about women. Why would he kill Linda and keep Julia alive?"

"I don't know," she said. "But she's alive. I can feel it."

"You had a feeling about Welch, too, and you were wrong."

She couldn't deny that. Did she feel that Julia was alive because she wanted so much for it to be true? Even Chief Stout would have no faith in her after this.

"Marty," he said roughly, "you have to promise me you won't take any more chances like you did tonight."

"I don't know..." Her voice broke.

"Let the police take care of it, honey. We're doing all there is to do."

Maybe he was right. She knew the wise thing would be to let the police handle it, but she couldn't stop worrying about Julia. She felt as though she had a special responsibility to find her. She clung to Walker. "Can you stay a while?"

"I shouldn't." But already his hands were burning on her waist and hips.

She clutched him tighter. "Please."

In a single movement, he stood and lifted her against him. He carried her through the house to the bedroom. There was a desperation in him, she knew it came from the fear he had felt when he realized what she'd done.

He set her on her feet beside the bed and threw off his jacket. Then he pressed her down on the bed with a sudden kiss. His hands roamed restlessly, as though he had to feel all of her, to make sure she was whole and safe.

She slid her hands around him, caressing the firmness of muscle under the khaki. His hands cradled her cheeks, his thumbs stroking at the corners of her willing lips, and he lifted her face to his.

The instant his hungry mouth crushed hers, passionate need gripped her. A moment before she had wanted comfort and assurance. Now she wanted—needed—sensual satiation. His tongue moved between her lips, and she trembled with the erotic awareness that this man, and no other, could give her such pleasure, and that her body could give him the pleasure he so desperately needed as well.

When at last he raised his head, she was on fire. Her eyes darkening, she reached for the front of his shirt and undid the buttons. "I want to feel your body next to mine."

"Marty," he gasped and she saw the burning passion in his eyes and heard the tortured intake of his breath. Between the two of them, they tore their clothes away. And then he bent over her and looked at the swell of her breasts with eyes glazed with desire. "You're all I think about," he said in a tortured whisper. "You've become more important to me than my life."

His coppery hair was tousled and somehow that made him look vulnerable. Behind his eyes leaped the fire that was raging in him. The bones of his face looked stark, chiseled. She put her hands up to his face. You are dearer to me than the whole world, she thought. These bones, the rough texture of your skin is exactly as it should be to arouse in me this wild madness. I will always remember you like this, always. Briefly she was overcome by melancholy, as if this was goodbye.

"I love you," he said.

As he spoke the words, he entered her, and the pleasure was exquisite. Her heart twitched, and she wondered if she had heard the words or only dreamed them. "No one has ever made me feel this way," she whispered, and tears stood in her eyes.

He was motionless in her, trembling, and his rough hand stroked her hair and breast and arm. "I will make you love me back," he growled. He moved in her then and the feeling was too deep for words to express. She tried to say his name, but her need was so great it was a deluge, flooding her, choking her.

His deep voice in her ear was hoarse, shaken. "I need this, Marty. I need you to need me. Tell me what you're feeling now. Let me hear you say it, Marty, please, please..."

Her body was moving with his now, caught in the rhythm he created; and she was shaking. "Yes...oh, yes..." But she could say no more.

"I can feel you trembling," he whispered. "That's it, my love. Pour yourself out for me."

She cried out as she reached the peak, and her body surrendered completely and the deep, shattering response racked her, drowned her and left her empty and weak.

Walker, feeling her surrender, lost himself in her. His body shook as the final release came, and he cried out her name.

She had poured him a cup of fresh coffee when he came out of the bathroom, dressed in his uniform and jacket once more. She was wearing a blue robe that turned her eyes the same soft color, and she smiled as she handed him the cup. She then brought her own cup to the table. "Sit down here with me."

Standing, he blew on the hot coffee and sipped carefully. "I have to get to work. I told Welch I'd be back after I talked to you." He pulled a chair out and lowered himself into it.

There was a momentary pause. "Is he going to sue me?"

His eyes admired her beauty, and he smiled. "No, I'll think of something to tell him. I'll get him to drop it, somehow."

"Thank you."

"Marty. Did you understand what I told you when we were making love?"

She knew what he was referring to, but she only said brightly, "I'm not sure I could repeat it word for word, but I got the gist."

There was a momentary pause. "I love you, Marty. And I don't say that easily. I've never loved anyone like this before."

Her eyes were unreadable, but she smiled. "I know what you want me to say, Walker, but I can't. I don't love lightly. The only time I loved a man, it ended in such pain...."

His eyes were on his coffee cup as he lifted it to his mouth. After a moment he said, "The man you were engaged to? You never told me what happened."

"I told him I had precognition." She said it calmly to ease the grip of tears on her throat. "He decided I was a mental case and suggested I might become a fortune teller." She gave a brittle little laugh.

He didn't laugh with her. He merely looked at her, his eyes full of understanding. But there was hurt, too, because she couldn't say she loved him. "You've told me all about yourself, and I'm still here, aren't I?" he asked gently.

"Yes, you're here—for now."

He set his cup down and got to his feet. He stood, looking down at her for a long moment. "I don't give up easily. You're worth waiting for."

She didn't reply. She couldn't because she knew the words would catch in her throat.

He came around the table and she realized he was going to kiss her. His mouth covered hers, and it was a quick, hot kiss full of yearning and emotional need. Then he lifted his head and said, "Let's go somewhere tomorrow night. You decide, and I'll call you in the morning."

"All right." Mercifully, she could speak in a relatively even voice. "Thank you for—everything. I feel much better now."

Her words made him smile, and then he was gone.

He hesitated outside the basement door. Was he making a mistake?

I just want to take a real bath, in a tub.

He'd thought about it all day. He knew that washing with a cloth dipped in a plastic dishpan wasn't as good as getting in a bathtub, no matter how thoroughly you scrubbed. On the other hand, there were still people in the world who bathed in a river only three or four times a year. Rita wasn't used to that kind of life, of course. He'd bought her some underwear and jeans and given her two of his old shirts, and he brought her the dishpan full of warm water every morning with a bar of soap. She still wasn't satisfied, though.

I can't imagine anything nicer than sliding down until the water covers me up to my chin. I could wash my hair much better, too.

He had taken the precaution of nailing heavy boards over the bathroom window. Rita swore that she remembered him, but sometimes when he looked at her, in the split second before she knew he was doing it, there was an expression on her face of—what? Despair, sometimes. And fear, too. Yesterday he thought he saw a flare of hatred in her eyes in that tiny instant before she realized he was watching her.

You can stand outside the door the whole time. I'll hurry. Don't you believe me?

She couldn't get out the window, he was sure of that. But what if she went crazy and started to scream? It wasn't beyond the realm of possibility. Rita had changed in the last seven years, so much that he felt he didn't even know her sometimes. There was no closeness between them now, even though she tried to pretend she felt the same about him. What had their mother told her to make her so suspicious and afraid? No, he'd better not think about their mother.

"Hey, are you out there?"

That was another thing. She had never once called him by his name. He didn't think she remembered it. How could she remember him and not his name? He tried not to let that upset him too much because he knew it was possible to block out memories that were too dreadful to remember. Hadn't he blocked out much of his childhood? Being tied to the bed and whipped and burned...

No! He would not remember.

He clenched his hands into tight fists until they hurt, then slowly relaxed. There, that was better. Yes, it was possible to block out unpleasant memories. But the thing that troubled him about Rita was, why would she have to block out anything about him? She had loved him when they were children. She had tried to shield him from their mother, even lied to protect him. Once in the middle of the night she had let him crawl under her bed to hide and, when their mother came storming into the room, swore she hadn't seen him since supper. Rita had always looked so sweet and innocent. That's why their mother could never tell when she was lying.

Now he'd put his finger on another thing that bothered him. If Rita could make their mother believe lies, couldn't she pull the same trick on him? Maybe she really didn't remember him at all. Indecision exhausted him. He'd been vacillating all day and felt as though he'd worked ten hours of hard labor. Actually, he had been unemployed for four months and was living on unemployment compensation.

Well, if he was going to do it, he had to do it now. Before the neighbors came home from wherever they'd gone. If she screamed, nobody would be able to hear her, not before he could haul her back down to the basement, anyway. He pulled a key from his pocket and opened the door.

"Are you ready to go upstairs for your bath?"

She was sitting on the cot and jumped up eagerly as he spoke. She was losing her color down here, as though the dark basement were draining her blood. She was losing weight, too, he thought, and she didn't have any extra to lose. It made him feel bad to see her so pale and skinny.

"Yes, almost ready." She grabbed a pair of jeans from the end of the cot and a clean pair of panties.

He went ahead of her up the stairs. On the landing, he waited until she was beside him, then linked his arm through hers.

"You don't have to hold on to me. I'm not going anywhere." She was holding back slightly, her gaze darting around the dining room, and coming to rest on the stack of bills on the chair next to the kitchen door.

Then they were in the kitchen, and he said, "Why don't you ever call me by my name?"

"I do."

"No, you never have."

She looked up at him in that studying way she had. "Robert." She watched his face and amended, "Bob, I mean."

So she did know. "You used to call me Bobby."

"I thought maybe you were too old for Bobby now."

"Bob's okay." He was remembering that stack of bills, the envelopes with his name on them. Could she have read one of them as they passed? She was looking all around again, as though she were trying to memorize as many details as possible. "The bathroom's this way."

"I was thinking—Bob. I've got lots of clothes in my room at the dorm. Couldn't you go over there and ask my roommate to pack a suitcase for me? Kate would be glad to—" He stopped walking; he stared at her. She stared back and there was definitely fear in her eyes now. "Of course, if you'd rather not... What are you doing? No, please!"

He was dragging her back toward the kitchen and through the dining room and into the hall. She was trying to pull away, crying now.

"Please—Bob, I won't say another word. Let me take a bath, please!"

He was too angry. He had to get her back downstairs and lock the door. He had to get out of the house for a little while. "Do you think I'm stupid?"

he snarled. "Do you?" He pulled so hard he almost jerked her off her feet.

They had reached the stairs. He didn't even break stride as he started down. She stumbled against him, and he hauled her upright and went on. He pulled her through the door and shoved her on the cot. She lay there, curled into a ball, whimpering.

"You've been lying!" he railed. "You don't remember me. You don't want to stay here. You want me to go to your roommate! So she can call somebody, send them to find you!" He stood there, shaking in outrage. He had tried to please her, and she had interpreted his act of kindness as weakness. She had taken him for a fool.

Suddenly he remembered how it had felt when he closed his hands around the other girl's neck—Linda Niles, that's the name he'd read in the paper. Seeing Rita lying there, cowering, made him want to hurt her.

He had to get out of there.

He backed across the room and through the door, slamming it behind him. His key grated in the lock. He started up the stairs. He had to have some fresh air.

"Bob, let me out. Please..."

He could still hear her crying, even when he was a block away from the house. He covered his ears and shook his head. No, he only imagined it. Nobody could hear her through those thick basement walls. It wasn't possible.

He threw his head back and gulped down great breaths of air. The temperature was near freezing, and he was in his shirt sleeves, but he hardly noticed. All he could think about was what a narrow escape he'd had. For a moment his hands had actually been reaching for her, wanting to curl around her neck. He'd come that close to living up to all the lies his mother had told Rita about him. He'd better stay away from the house for a while. Not go back until he was tired enough to sleep.

He started to run.

Chapter 10

Marty couldn't sleep. She wandered through the house, her nerves jumping at every faint sound. She had told Walker she felt better, but as soon as he had gone she realized she didn't. Too much had happened tonight: Welch surprising her at his house and then reporting her to the police; Walker's anger, his reminder that her "feeling" about Welch had been wrong, and then his declaration of love.

To top things off, her throat felt raspy. She thought she was coming down with something. Probably caused by being chilled for hours, sitting in the cold car. And all for nothing.

The telephone rang. She wondered if Welch had gotten her phone number and was calling to give her a piece of his mind. For a moment, she was tempted not to answer.

The phone kept ringing and, finally, she snatched up the receiver. "Hello."

"Did I wake you?" It was Walker.

"No."

"What took you so long to answer?"

"I was afraid it was Welch," she admitted.

"Don't worry about that. I went out there and talked to him. He's agreed not to press charges."

Relief washed over her. "How did you manage that?"

"I told him you thought somebody else lived in the house, and that you were embarrassed and sorry and wouldn't bother him again."

All of that was true, but she resented hearing it from Walker. It was almost as if he wanted to underline the fact that she had been wrong about Welch, to suggest that her "feelings" were never to be trusted.

"Marty, I've been looking through the files on the Niles and Allman cases, trying to sketch out a psychological profile of the killer. What kind of man would kidnap and murder young women?"

He sounded so businesslike. Had she imagined the lovemaking and endearments only an hour ago? Everything about this night seemed confusing. Maybe she had a fever and was slightly delirious.

"You said it yourself," she remarked finally. "He's got a hang-up about women."

"But what would give a man that kind of hang-up?"

She closed her eyes. They felt dry and scratchy. She tried to center her mind on Walker's question. "I know it's a cliché to blame the mother, but clichés are clichés because they grow out of a common reality. Some woman, anyway, has hurt him. He's deeply scarred emotionally. Whatever she did, he interpreted it as complete and total rejection."

"This woman, then, doesn't necessarily have to be his mother. It could be a wife or girlfriend."

"Possibly. But emotional traumas ingrained deeply enough to make him act out his hostility so violently were probably inflicted in childhood and have been festering for years. It's only a guess, of course, but I'd say it's more likely his mother or a mother figure who caused him to hate women. Very often such acting out involves rape."

"Yeah, that's true in most of these cases I've read about. But there was no evidence that Linda Niles was sexually assaulted. I wonder why."

"Any number of reasons. He could be impotent, for one thing."

"As a result of the same childhood experiences?"

"Possibly."

"Could somebody this troubled be cured with psychological counseling?"

Marty smiled wanly and pressed thumb and index finger against her eyelids in an attempt to ease the burning sensation. "Cured isn't exactly psychological terminology. He could possibly be helped to understand the source of his hostility and learn to deal with it in more acceptable ways. It would take a lot of desire and determination on the part of the patient, and it might require years of counseling."

Walker was silent for several moments, and she supposed he was making notes. Finally he asked, "Do you have any patients at the clinic who fit the profile?''

Marty was unprepared for the question, and it was an instant before the connotations occurred to her. This was what the whole conversation had been leading up to. Walker had led her cleverly, first making her feel obligated because he'd gotten Welch to forget pressing charges, then flattering her by asking her professional opinion. No, *first*, he'd weakened her with his lovemaking and, then, he'd told her he loved her. She stood there, staggered by the implications her mind was coming up with.

She couldn't think of a patient who fit the profile, but that wasn't the point. She wasn't prepared to deal with this now; she was ill. "You're asking me to betray a professional confidence, Walker."

"Don't give me that." His tone brushed aside all professional confidences with one swoop. He had undoubtedly run into the same barrier before. To him, it was simply an argument that was invalid in a criminal case. Well, hadn't she known from the beginning that cops and psychologists were worlds apart?

"I have to go, Walker. I don't feel well. I think I have the flu."

"Honey, I'm sorry. Why didn't you say something sooner? I'll come by when I get off work. Is there anything I can bring you?"

He sounded contrite, but it was too late to erase her growing confusion. "No, I don't want to give you my germs. I've got aspirin and orange juice. That's all I need."

"Well, if you're sure . . ."

"I'm sure, Walker. Good night."

She found a thermometer and discovered that her temperature was 101—and rising, judging by the way she felt. She swallowed three aspirin tablets and went to bed.

But not to sleep. The fever seemed to be burning the fantasies out of her brain. In spite of body aches and a splitting headache, she was seeing things clearly for the first time in weeks. The more she thought about it, the more convinced she was that Walker's basic opinion of her remained the same as it had been the first time they met. He put no credence in her dreams. None. To him she was mistaken, possibly even neurotic. But he wasn't above using their personal relationship to undermine her responsibility to professional clients. Oh, he found her physically attractive, she'd known that the first morning at the police station.

Was there anything between them besides sex?

She wrestled with the question for a long time without finding a satisfactory answer. Eventually she fell into a fretful, feverish sleep.

Walker was back on the day shift again. Monday morning, he came to the station after one of the worst weekends of his life. Marty was refusing to see him. She'd been sick all weekend—or said she was. At first he'd believed her when she said she didn't want him to come to the house because she didn't want to infect him. But when he talked to her on the phone, she sounded so distant that, finally, he began to suspect it was more than the flu.

Now he was sure of it.

Sunday night, he's asked her point-blank what was wrong, threatened to go to her house and force his way in if she didn't tell him.

"Walker," she said, "I just don't think this is going to work."

She could have been talking about the Allman case, but the subdued, desolate tone of her voice told him she wasn't. She was talking about them. She didn't think the two of them together was going to work.

Marty had gone on to say that she needed space, time to think it through. There was no room for argument in her voice. Walker felt as if his whole world was coming down around his head. He had awakened several times during the night with the same question resounding in his mind: What had he done?

It must be that he'd said he loved her. Marty had made it quite plain that she wasn't ready to fall in love with anyone. But he had said he was willing to wait. He found it difficult to believe that his declaration of love had scared her so badly she didn't even want to see him. Yet what else could it be?

His entire adult life had been one of lighthearted relationships with women. A lot of laughs, and no strings. He had looked at Jess and Rose's enduring love for each other and wondered if he'd ever want to settle down with one woman, forever. Now that he had found that one woman, she didn't want him! How ironic that this particular state of affairs had never occurred to him. Women had always wanted more than he did from a relationship. He was the one who got bored and called it quits. Now the tables were turned, and it hurt like hell!

Nelda had decided to make the coffee this morning. It was one small ray of sunshine in an otherwise dark universe. Walker was helping himself to his first cup of the day when Jess appeared at his office door and gestured for Walker to join him.

When Walker was seated, Jess pointed to a report on his desk. "What's this about Marty Newland trespassing out on Thirty-fifth Street?" Jess bent over the desk, peering over the top of his glasses. "Window-peeking, according to Phillips's notes." He looked at Walker with an incredulous expression.

"It's not what it sounds like," Walker grumbled. "Everything's cleared up. I took care of it."

Jess sat down, leaning back in his chair. "So Phillips told me. Said you insisted on following up. Phillips couldn't figure why you were so adamant. I guess he doesn't know about you and Marty."

Walker shrugged and took a swallow of coffee.

"You talked Welch into forgetting the complaint?"

Walker nodded.

"I'm curious. How'd you do that?"

"I explained it was all a mistake."

Jess put his hands behind his head. "Uh-huh. What kind of mistake?"

Walker sighed and said reluctantly, "Marty got the idea that the man she saw in her dream with Julia Allman was into physical fitness. So she'd been hanging around the health clubs, looking for the guy. She saw Welch leaving one of the clubs last week. She thought he looked like the man in her dream. She got his name and found his address in the phone book.''

Jess looked slightly stunned. ''I'm beginning to see the light. She wanted to see Welch's kitchen.''

''Right,'' Walker muttered. ''It wasn't anything like the one in her dream, by the way.'' He shook his head. ''I had no idea what she was up to, or I'd have stopped her before it went so far.''

Jess's eyes twinkled. ''Would you now? Marty might have had something to say about that. I got the idea she's pretty independent.''

Walker slouched deeper into his chair. ''Yeah,'' he said with great bitterness.

Jess eyed him ruminatively. ''Problems?''

''She won't see me, Jess.'' Walker downed the last of his coffee and crushed the Styrofoam cup in his hand. Gazing at the destroyed cup, he blurted, ''Hell, I don't know what to do. I'll never understand women.''

''Not women, one woman,'' Jess said sagely. ''You're in love with her.''

Walker was too depressed to summon the energy for denial, so he remained morosely silent.

''Have you told her how you feel?''

Walker grunted, ''That was my big mistake.''

''Now wait a minute.'' Jess leaned forward, his elbows on the desk. ''It's never a mistake to tell a woman you're in love with her.''

''In this case, it was, Jess. Don't ask me why, but it scared her. The only reason I can figure is that she doesn't feel the same about me.''

Jess pursed his lips. "I wouldn't be so sure about that. Rose commented about the way Marty acted at our house the other Sunday. Rose thinks she's falling for you, and Rose is rarely wrong in these things."

"Rose is a romantic. At the very least, Marty's feelings are ambivalent. She says she needs space to think things through."

Jess picked up a pen and tapped it on the desk. "You know, Walker, you've made no secret of the fact that you don't believe in Marty's psychic ability. How do you think that makes her feel?"

Suddenly restless, Walker got to his feet and thrust his hands into his trouser pockets. He walked to the window and stared out for a moment. "She was wrong about Welch. Doesn't that cast doubt on her psychic ability?"

"I don't know. Where is it written psychics have to be right every time?"

Walker turned around and wandered toward the door. "I won't lie to her, Jess. Marty will have to take me as I am, or not at all. That's the only way it would work."

"That goes both ways."

Walker threw him a perplexed look.

"Turn that around," Jess advised, "and ask yourself if you're willing to take Marty as she is. Be honest with yourself, now. Wouldn't you like it a lot better if Marty had never had any of those unexplainable experiences? This skepticism of yours—what it must boil down to in Marty's mind is that you don't have any faith in her."

Walker opened the door. "I thought you were my friend. Whose side are you on, anyway?"

"Yours."

Walker left, feeling nevertheless that somebody he'd depended on had let him down.

Several times during the day, he thought about what Jess had said, becoming more frustrated by the hour.

Marty went home from work Monday, feeling so weak she was trembling. She'd put in a full day at the clinic; it wasn't until midafternoon that she'd realized she hadn't regained her full strength after her weekend illness. Even so, she was grateful for her full schedule; it left her little time to think about Walker.

When she turned into her own driveway at five-thirty, she wanted only to crawl into bed. But first she had to eat and bathe. She could get to bed by seven-thirty, she calculated as she let herself into the bungalow. Twelve hours' sleep would go a long way toward restoring her strength.

She sat down to a soup-and-milk dinner at her kitchen table just as the telephone rang. She half stood to reach it and sank back down in her chair. "Hello."

"Are you feeling better?"

Walker. He was making this very difficult for her. Why couldn't he leave her be? "Some."

"Did you go to work today?"

"Yes. I'm going to eat and go to bed early."

"Oh." He cleared his throat. "I was hoping I could see you tonight."

Hearing his subdued voice almost made her forget her problems with Walker. Tired as she was, she was sorely tempted to tell him to come over. She was so weak and confused. She badly needed Walker to hold her and tell her everything would be all right. The invitation was on the tip of her tongue before she could stop herself.

Nothing had changed. Letting Walker come to the house would only encourage him to believe she wanted to go back to the way they had been. As things stood, it was better not to see him. "I'm really too tired to see you tonight, Walker."

"What about tomorrow night?"

"I don't think so."

She heard his heavy intake of breath. "Okay, Marty. Good night, then."

The discouragement in his voice made her want to take back what she'd said. If he'd given her another few moments, she might have; but there was an abrupt click on the other end of the line, and then she heard the dial tone.

After dinner she took a long, leisurely bath. Before getting into the tub, she studied her reflection in the large bathroom mirror. The heater hadn't had time to warm the room yet, and she could see tiny goose bumps on her arms. She stared at her pale, slender body, aware of what she considered its faults—breasts not as large as she would like, hips a little too full. She knew, from the women she'd counseled, that it was a rare female who was completely satisfied with her physical appearance. She wondered if men were as critical of themselves as women.

She doubted it. She couldn't imagine Walker worrying over the size of his shoulders or the color of his hair. No, Walker was at ease in his body. When she was with him, some of that self-acceptance rubbed off on her. When he made love to her, she felt beautiful and desirable. When he cupped her breast or caressed her hip...

She shivered and turned away from the mirror. She soaked in the warm, bubbly bathwater, her head resting on the tub's rim. She tried to make her mind go blank, but the memories of Walker's lovemaking were too potent. Heat that had nothing to do with the steamy water stole through her. How long would it take her to forget him?

How had she managed to delude herself into thinking she could have a safe, surface relationship with Walker? There was nothing safe—or surface—about him. He wouldn't be easy to forget.

Sighing, she shifted and the soapy bubbles moved against her breasts, reminding her of Walker's hungry caresses. Behind her closed eyelids she could see his unruly red hair, his chiseled features, his hazel eyes darkened to umber by passion. It was no effort at all to remember his hands, hard and hot, roaming her body, stoking her desire.

Groaning, she sat up and reached for a thick, thirsty washcloth. She scrubbed her body vigorously, imagining that she was scrubbing away the memories of Walker's boyish grin, the sweet words he whispered in her ear when they made love, the way he touched her when they went out together, as if to broadcast his possession of her. There was no doubt in her mind that she loved him. And maybe he really believed he loved her, too. But it was a love that couldn't survive. No love, not rooted in complete and implicit trust on both sides, could last. Danny had taught her that.

During that long night, Walker's frustration turned to anger fueled by devastated masculine ego. Obviously Marty had decided to break off their relationship completely. No explanations, no discussion. Just the end, period.

After he'd bared his soul and admitted that he loved her. He kept coming back to that, stirring and restirring his humiliation like picking the scab off a cut. He hadn't had much practice at handling rejection. The pain was worse than he could have imagined, and there wasn't a damned thing he could do about it.

Marty had decided they were through. Well, if that's the way she wanted it, he'd have to live with it. Thank God he had his work, and with the Niles-Allman case, he had his hands more than full.

Just how full was brought home to him when he opened the morning paper at the breakfast table. "Citizens' Group Charges Police with Incompetence," the headline blared.

John Petree, head of the newly organized citizens' action group, Citizens for Tough Justice, has issued a statement charging the local police department with incompetence in their handling of the case involving the murder of Willow State coed, Linda Niles, and the disappearance of a second coed, Julia Allman. Petree's statement claims that repeated requests for a meeting between the group and Police Chief Jess Stout have

been ignored. "As Willow citizens and taxpay-
ers," Petree said, "we have a right to know what
is being done to solve the case. Chief Stout seems
more concerned with protecting his position until he can retire than with finding the murderer."
Petree's statement calls for immediate public dis-
closure as to whether the police have any suspects or evidence in the case and whether any
other criminal investigation agencies have been
contacted for help. "The police department's secrecy indicates to me that they haven't made any
progress at all," Petree said. "If that's the situation, what this town needs is a few resignations
from the force."

Leaving his breakfast untouched, Walker grabbed
the newspaper and his jacket and slammed out of the
house. Idiots, he fumed as he drove to the station, I'd
like to see them do any better than we've done! We're
understaffed and underpaid, but we're supposed to
take abuse from every crackpot on the street and work
miracles to boot!

Newspaper tightly folded and clamped under his
arm, Walker strode into the station. First, coffee.
Then, the chief's office. He came to a halt in front of
the coffee urn. It had obviously not been touched this
morning. His frustrated gaze swept over Nelda, who
was bent over the newspaper on her desk.

"Nelda," Walker barked as he stormed past on his
way to the chief's office, "would you mind getting off
your can and making the coffee?"

Nelda came to her feet and watched Walker stalking down the hall away from her. "Look, Dietrick," she called, "I'm sorry about that newspaper article, but don't take it out on me!" Walker didn't respond and, still grumbling, Nelda walked to the urn and removed yesterday's grounds.

Jess was alone in his office. Leaning back in his chair, he had the newspaper spread open on his knees.

Walker entered, sat down, and tossed his newspaper on the desk. "I thought I might get here before you saw it."

Jess looked over the top of his glasses and gave a humorless snort. "I had two calls from city councilmen before I left the house. Rainbolt read the whole front page to me. I was just reading it again to see if it was as bad as Rainbolt made it sound." Jess removed his glasses and pinched the bridge of his nose between thumb and forefinger. "I'm afraid it is."

"When we solved that string of burglaries last year, the editor buried the story on an inside page."

"Walker, Walker...don't expect justice from newspaper editors. Those burglars last year happened to be the sons of prominent businessmen."

"I hate city politics," Walker grumbled.

"You better get used to it if you're gonna stay on the force."

Walker waved a hand at the newspaper he'd thrown on the desk. "There might be a question about that. What'd the councilman say?"

"Oh, that maybe I ought to be thinking about retiring pretty soon, get out from under the pressure, let younger men take over. Rainbolt hinted we might need to bring a big city cop in on the case, somebody properly trained in murder investigations.''

''That spineless—''

Jess laughed. ''Rainbolt's under the gun, too. Said he'd had five calls from outraged citizens this morning already. Don't let it get to you, Walker. I'm not resigning under pressure. They'll have to fire me if they want me to leave before this case is closed.''

''If it ever is,'' Walker muttered.

''It'll break one of these days,'' Jess assured him, ''when we least expect it, probably. Keep the faith, Walker.''

Going to his own office a few minutes later, Walker wondered if Jess was as sure about that as he sounded.

He was sure going to do his part to support Jess. Now that Marty wouldn't see him, he could spend all his waking hours on the case. Every cloud has a silver lining, he told himself grimly.

Chapter 11

"You should have stayed in bed today."

Jerry had carried his midmorning coffee into Marty's office. He made himself comfortable in the chair recently vacated by Fern Small, who was still dazed by the unexpected desertion of her boyfriend, Charley, over the weekend. "He moved out Saturday, Miss Newland," Fern had said, tears streaming down her face, "and he wouldn't tell me where he was going. I haven't heard from him. It's over, I just know it. Oh . . . what am I gonna do?"

Accept it, live with it one day at a time, Marty had said—keep busy, go out with other men. Marty had felt like the world's biggest hypocrite as she listened to the glib advice falling off her tongue. Since breaking up with Walker, she was painfully aware of how much harder advice was to take than to give. She wasn't handling her own situation at all well. Determined to get a long night's sleep the previous night, she had nevertheless lain awake for hours, remembering every minute she had spent with Walker, hearing the things he had said to her, and fighting a deep need to pick up the phone and call merely to hear his voice.

"Do I look that bad?" Marty asked Jerry now. She took a sip of coffee Dotty had set on her desk a few moments earlier and leaned back in her chair. Jerry looked rakishly handsome in a bulky white crew-neck sweater, brown tweed trousers and shining mahogany leather loafers.

"I've seen you look a lot better. I don't think you've recovered from the flu. You shouldn't push yourself."

"I haven't had any fever for twenty-four hours," Marty said. "I just didn't sleep well last night. But I'd rather be working than at home with time on my hands."

"Sleeplessness usually means one of two things," he said with a grin. "Which was it, worry or a guilty conscience?"

"Neither," Marty said too quickly. "It was merely one of those nights when I wasn't sleepy. Don't tell me you don't have one now and then."

"Hardly ever. I'm almost always wrung out when I get ready to go to sleep." The sly twinkle in his eyes suggested he was contemplating the many women who were more than willing to contribute to his physical exhaustion.

Marty raised an eyebrow. "Bragging or complaining, Jerry?"

"Just stating the facts, ma'am." Smugness was one of Jerry's less attractive traits. "What you need, my dear, is somebody to show you a good time, take your mind off your troubles."

Marty smiled. "Are you volunteering?"

Jerry took a swallow of coffee, then gave her a jaunty wink. "I'm available."

Recalling her insistence that Fern Small must be kept busy, Marty hesitated before responding. Maybe she should try a bit of her own advice. "Exactly what did you have in mind?"

"Dinner at the Silver Spoon tonight," Jerry said smoothly, "followed by dancing. A pretty good combo plays golden oldies there from eight to midnight."

To Marty's surprise, the suggestion had a certain appeal. Anything would be better than spending another long, lonely evening at home. She and Jerry should be able to find plenty to talk about. She would have an entire evening free of painful memories. It would be a first step in getting over Walker. "You've got yourself a date, Jer." His double-take made her laugh. "You didn't expect me to say yes, did you? You were just clowning around."

He shook his head. "I didn't expect a yes, but I wasn't kidding." He studied her intently. "I must have asked you out a dozen times before, and you've said no. Why is this time different?"

Marty shrugged. "If you want to weasel out, Jer, just say so."

"No," he said hastily. He got up and tossed his empty Styrofoam cup into her wastebasket. "I'm

going to get out of here before you change your mind.
I'll pick you up at seven-thirty."

As he reached the door, she said, "Just so we understand each other, Jerry. I accepted an invitation for
dinner and dancing. That's it."

He looked over his shoulder and grimaced. "Aw,
come on, Marty. I've never forced myself on a woman
in my life. Give me a little credit."

She waved him away and opened Fern Small's file
to make notes on the morning's session.

The Silver Spoon was a supper club on the highway
a couple of miles north of Willow. Marty had never
been there before; from its location—outside the city
limits—and exterior—unadorned, except for a neon
sign, and skimpily landscaped—she had assumed it
was just another beer joint. But as soon as she entered with Jerry, she realized she'd misjudged the
place. The interior was attractive with blue carpeting
and dark-stained tables placed far enough apart to
provide privacy. Several well-executed oil paintings by
local artists adorned the walls and there was a small
stage containing a piano and several chairs and music
stands at one end of the room. The lighting was just
dim enough to be intimate.

The hostess exchanged friendly greetings with Jerry,
who was evidently a frequent customer, and showed
them to a table near the small dance floor in front of
the raised platform.

It seemed odd to have Jerry cupping her elbow as
they crossed the restaurant and holding her chair for
her. She could banter with him indefinitely at the office, but this wasn't the same. He wore an expensively

tailored gray, vested suit with a gray-and-red-striped tie and shirt of pristine white. Marty had deliberately chosen a simple skirt and blouse and felt underdressed by comparison. She was already wondering if accepting Jerry's invitation had been a mistake.

She looked around the restaurant, but saw no one she knew. "This is my first time here."

Jerry sat down, facing her. "Oh? Where does Walker Dietrick take you?"

Walker's name, dropped into the conversation without warning, jolted Marty. She hadn't been aware that Jerry knew she'd been seeing Walker. Then she remembered that Walker had come to the clinic once to take her to lunch. She smoothed her napkin on her lap as she tried to recover from her surprise. "Nowhere."

"Hmm," he mused, "since when?"

The evening wasn't going as planned. Going out with Jerry was supposed to take her mind off Walker. She opened one of the menus the hostess had left. "Could we talk about something else, please?"

After gazing at her thoughtfully for another moment, Jerry perused his own menu. They ordered and then Jerry told an amusing story about his pennypinching landlady, who let herself into Jerry's apartment when he was at work and turned the gas furnace to a lower setting. "It was like Alaska in there today when I got home," Jerry told her. "I asked Mrs. Wilson if she'd seen anybody messing around my place, and she swore she'd been in her apartment all day and hadn't heard anybody going upstairs. I'm going to get a new lock installed. She won't be able to say anything about it without giving herself away."

Marty was thankful he seemed willing to let the subject of Walker drop, and she began to relax. "Tricky, Jerry. You might find yourself paying your own gas bill, though."

The members of the combo had come on stage and were warming up. By the time their waitress brought their entrees, the combo was playing a medley of romantic forties and fifties melodies. A young woman in a black sequined gown came to the microphone and began to sing in a deep, sultry voice.

Marty was unprepared for the sadness that swept over her as she listened to the music. They seemed to have exhausted the subject of Jerry's landlady. She tried to shut out the music and said brightly, "Do you still see that English teacher from the college?"

"Occasionally. Why?"

"She seems nice, and she's very pretty. The two of you make a handsome couple."

"Tammy wants to get married and have babies. Immediately, if not sooner. She's thirty and thinks her prime childbearing years are running out."

Marty buttered a dinner roll. "Do you have something against marriage and children?" Jerry, she knew, was thirty-one, and she assumed everybody would like to have a family eventually.

"Nope, at the right time and with the right woman."

"Tammy isn't the right woman?"

"She might be if she weren't so earnest about home and hearth. I'm not ready to give up my freedom for a few years yet, and I don't think Tammy's willing to wait that long. Lately she's been dating one of the English professors. He strikes me as the pipe-and-slippers type.''

"You don't sound bothered, so you can't be in love with her."

He smiled. "I've been in love too many times to count. Tammy won't be the last."

Marty eyed him, wondering what he was really thinking underneath that suave, man-about-town facade. "You make it sound so easy."

"What, falling in and out of love? It is."

"Infatuation, maybe, but not real love."

He laughed softly. "You're an expert on the subject?"

"No." She cut a piece of her veal. "I'm certainly not that." She brought the meat to her mouth and chewed slowly.

Jerry watched her in a calculating sort of way. "Have you ever been in love?"

Marty laughed shortly. "Not as many times as you, apparently."

"How many?" he persisted.

She tried to sound casual. "Oh, once or twice. I was engaged before I moved to Willow."

"That's once. Now you're in love with Dietrick, aren't you?"

Marty put her fork down. "I told you I'm no longer seeing him."

"That's not what I asked. What happened, Marty? Did he hurt you?"

She felt heat creeping up her throat and reached for her water glass. She almost missed the glass and tipped it, spilling water, before she grabbed it and set it upright again. "Oh, dear...."

Jerry motioned for their waitress. "Are you finished eating?"

"Yes." All she wanted now was to go home and be by herself.

"Would you like dessert?"

"No."

"Let's dance while the waitress cleans this up. Then we'll have coffee before we go."

She couldn't think of a reasonable excuse not to dance with Jerry. So she let him lead her to the dance floor and, after the slightest hesitation, went into his arms. He was a smooth dancer. He held her neither too tightly nor too loosely. She could feel the mere suggestion of his chest and thighs as they moved together in time with the slow music. She had never danced with Walker, and yet being in Jerry's arms caused her mind to be flooded with the memories she was trying to hold at bay. Walker was taller than Jerry, his shoulders broader, his hands larger. Although she doubted that Walker was as accomplished a dancer as Jerry, she couldn't help comparing the two, and Jerry came off second-best. The music stopped and, relieved, Marty started to leave the dance floor. But the combo started another tune and Jerry grabbed her hand and pulled her back into his arms.

If it had been any other song, she could have kept her composure until Jerry dropped her at the bungalow. But it was the song she and Walker had listened to on the car radio on their second date, when he had taken her to Altus for dinner—a song filled with broken hearts and lonely nights and lost love. When they reached Walker's house, he had made love to her for the first time. . . .

Without any warning, Marty's eyes filled with tears and when she tried to blink them away they spilled over and trickled down her cheeks. To make it even more embarrassing, Jerry chose that moment to hold her away from him and look down at her.

She gazed back at him helplessly and, withdrawing her hand from his, wiped her cheeks. "This is so silly. I don't know what's wrong with me. I guess I'm not fully recovered from my flu, after all."

"Yeah," Jerry said, his tone heavy with irony, "that must be it." They had stopped dancing and were standing at the edge of the dance floor.

"I'm embarrassed. Would you mind very much if I asked you to take me home now?"

He pulled a handkerchief from his coat pocket and gently blotted her cheeks. "No, I'll get the check," he said kindly. "You get our coats and meet me in the foyer."

By the time Jerry joined her in the foyer, she had succeeded in banishing her tears. Neither of them spoke until Jerry stopped the car in Marty's driveway.

He switched off the engine, then turned to her and said, "I don't mind being used to help a woman forget another man, Marty, but you might have told me."

Astonished, she stared at his handsome face, which was clearly illuminated by the yard lamp. "That isn't true, Jerry."

"Isn't it?"

Honesty forced her to admit that perhaps there was partial truth in his accusation. She sighed, "I only wanted to have an enjoyable evening and not think—"

She broke off and he let the silence hang between them for a moment before he said, "Not think about Dietrick? Yes, I know."

She looked away from him. "I'm sorry."

He climbed out of the car and went around to open her door. Throwing his arm around her shoulders, he walked with her to the door. "It's okay, Marty," he said companionably. "Just let me know what my role is next time. If I'd known tonight, I wouldn't have bothered with a romantic setting. I could have worn jeans and taken you to McDonald's."

He was teasing her, trying to make her feel better. She looked up at him and her spirits lifted. On her front porch, she got her key and opened the door. Then, on an impulse, she kissed his cheek before stepping inside. "Thanks, Jer. You're a good friend."

But melancholy returned the moment she heard Jerry driving away, and she was crying again.

Walker had worked overtime, leaving the station at seven, having accepted Hemphill's suggestion that they stop nearby for a beer. He nursed two beers for an hour and, after Hemphill left, ordered a cheeseburger. He didn't look forward to going home. A friend from his high school days in Willow came into the restaurant and Walker insisted that he sit with him. They reminisced for another hour. But eventually Walker couldn't put off going home any longer.

He didn't consciously plan to drive by Marty's house en route, but when he realized he'd taken the wrong turn at a stoplight he didn't turn back. He wondered if she was missing him as much as he missed her. God, he hoped so.

He reached Marty's street and slowed so that he could get a good look at her house as he passed. If the lights were on, maybe he'd stop...

He had reached the house next door when he noticed the unfamiliar car in her driveway. Then he saw them in the light from the yard lamp—Marty and Jerry Macomber. Macomber had his arm around her. Walker accelerated and, craning for a last look over his shoulder, he saw what looked like a single shadow on the dark porch instead of two, as though they were kissing. Then he was too far away to see anything more, but his imagination filled in the void with a vengeance.

He gripped the steering wheel so hard that pain shot through his fingers. His heart was hammering and drenching sweat had popped out all over his body. For a moment, he didn't even realize where he was. He could only remember what he'd seen.

Marty and Macomber together, kissing....

They must be inside the bungalow now....

Walker drew a long, shuddering breath, and released it in a deep sigh of despair.

Marty spent Thanksgiving Day alone. It wasn't the first time she had done so, but this year there was no contentment to be found in her solitude. Dotty had taken pity on Marty and offered an invitation to her parent's house for dinner. Marty had thanked her and declined. She didn't know with whom Jerry was spending the day. Since Tuesday night, they had spoken only briefly in passing. Jerry wouldn't ask her out again, she was sure, and she wasn't sorry. After the dismal failure their "date" had been, neither of them was inclined to try again.

Marty baked a hen and made cornbread dressing, a sweet potato casserole, and pumpkin pie, determined to make the day special, even though she would be alone. She wondered what Walker was doing. Would he spend the day with the Stouts? Maybe he was seeing another woman now and would be with her. That was a possibility she would have to accept. Missing Walker wasn't getting any easier, but she told herself it was only a matter of time until the memories would fade from her mind.

At six-thirty, she arranged her Thanksgiving meal on a tray and carried it to the living room. She found her favorite FM station on the radio, then settled down to eat and listen to the music. It was cold out. Snow had begun to fall thinly before the evening darkness made it impossible to see the flakes. The driving wind howling past the bungalow made her thankful she was warmly tucked inside.

She was halfway through her meal when the radio disc jockey said, "Here's a new song and a new artist

I think you're going to like, folks. Listen up, and let me know what you think.''

> ...my brain resounding with
> the words we left unsaid...
> The pain of longing echoes
> in my soul...

Marty listened and was filled with a sudden savage need for Walker, for the mere sight of him. Yes, she thought, I know all about the pain of longing. Do the memories ever go away?

> People speak to me
> and I reply
> with sounds that have
> no meaning anymore.

> ...the house looks as
> it always did before
> unmarred by wind and rain
> and dreams that die.

Marty dropped her fork and let her head fall back against the couch. She shut her eyes, thinking that the songwriter must have also lost someone he loved to have written so truly. Yesterday, when she came home from work, she had looked around her living room and thought, how can it look the same when I feel as if nothing will ever be right again?

Then she had begun to remember Walker, sprawled on the couch, dozing, his arms around her as she lay with her head resting on his shoulder. Walker sitting on the carpet in his stocking feet, as they played some board game and drank hot chocolate. Walker, lounging in the doorway to the dining room, grinning. She had been without him for a week now, and simply getting through the days seemed harder, not easier. As the song said, he hadn't left his mark on her house, he had left it on her. At this moment, the thought of him was a dead weight in her chest, a heaviness in her lower body, an ache in her arms and hands and breasts.

Marty switched off the radio, then carried her tray back to the kitchen. She rinsed the dishes she had used, put them in the dishwasher, covered and stored the remainder of her Thanksgiving meal in the refrigerator. There would be enough food for two or three evenings; she hadn't eaten much.

She wandered through the house, which was spotless from the thorough cleaning she had done that morning. She could find nothing to do. She paced the length of the bungalow from living room to kitchen, and back again. Her muscles felt bunched and tense, and she was aware of the pull of her jeans against her thighs as she paced. Her eyes were hot with unshed tears.

Suddenly she went to the living-room phone and laid her hand on the receiver. What would she say if she called? I miss you so much . . . I don't think I can stay sane without you. . . .

The loud knocking at her front door made her start violently. She whirled around and stared at the door.

The impatient knocking continued. "Marty!"

With a gasp, she went to the door, released the lock, and opened it.

He was dressed in jeans and his sheepskin jacket. His hair was tousled and his face ruddy from the blast of the cold wind. His eyes were red-rimmed, as though from strain or lack of sleep.

"Walker," she breathed as he opened the screen and stepped inside. His eyes were devouring her as he closed the door.

He swallowed convulsively and reached for her. He wrapped her in his arms and bent to kiss her, slowly, carefully, as though he feared a total release of his hunger would hurt her. In the first instant, his lips were cold from the wind, and then they were hot and seeking.

Marty drew back, shaking, filled with the upheaval of her emotions. It almost seemed as if her despairing thoughts had conjured him up. Sensing the urgency in him, she took a step away. "What are you doing here?" Her low voice cracked, and she put her hand to her throat to ease the tension there. Why was she asking stupid questions when moments ago she would have given anything for the sight of him? She needed a minute to think. If he kissed her again, there would be no thinking until it was too late.

"I couldn't stay away any longer," said Walker, his voice full of hunger and sadness. "I tried. Everything reminded me of you."

She sighed. "It was the same for me." She backed away another step because what she really wanted to do was throw herself into his arms. "I suppose we have to talk."

Walker shrugged off his jacket, took two strides, and pulled her roughly against him. "We can talk later. All I have to say now is that you don't have to love me. I have enough love for both of us." His big, rough hands came up to hold her face, and with a shuddery intake of breath he covered her mouth with his.

Instantly, she was overcome with a deluge of need. What was there to say that meant anything compared to this hopeless, helpless flood of longing? The solace of his sheltering arms, the warmth and hardness of his body against hers, the ravaging possession of his mouth, said far more than words could ever express. This was what she had dreamed of the past six nights, and thought it would never again be anything but a dream. Now it was happening, and she could think of nothing else.

She buried her fingers in the thick hair at the back of his head until the fingertips touched his scalp. With a moan, she pulled his head lower and moved her mouth from his to kiss the harsh angle of his jaw and chin and cheek, wherever she could reach.

He pulled her shirt from the waistband of her jeans and slid his hands underneath to touch her skin. Blindly, she fumbled his shirt buttons open and sought his warm flesh with her hungry hands. He unfastened her bra and pushed it aside. His hand closed over her breast, sending weakness melting through her, and her breath caught on a groan of need.

A fever of urgency flooded through her. She couldn't touch enough of him. Her hands and mouth had a raging need to caress the hair-roughened skin of his chest and thighs. "Come," she whispered and, clutching his hand, led him to her bedroom.

The lonely bed that had supported her restless, needing body the past six nights would not be lonely tonight. They began to undress each other, pausing again and again to bring their mouths together and drink of the sweet nectar they had denied themselves too long.

He lay down on the bed and pulled her on top of him. She felt the stretched muscles of his thighs, the thrusting hardness of his manhood, the crushing of her breasts against his chest, the pressure of his arms encircling her, and the intense heat suffusing her wherever his flesh touched hers. The fire in her blood leaped to meet the answering fire in him, and her mouth demanded sustenance as greedily as his.

She had forgotten how perfectly his hand fit her hips, how wonderful were his lingering caresses, how his kisses drowned her in pleasure and left her pleading for more. He showed her how dead her body had been without the nourishment only he could give.

Her response was electric. In an abandonment so unrestrained it shook them both, she gave him kiss for kiss, caress for caress, arching to offer herself to him completely.

Walker's senses were demolished by the power of the need he felt in her, and the hunger exploded and raged through him like wildfire. Groaning he rolled over and raised himself above her, and she guided him to her with eager clinging hands.

She gazed up at him in the darkening shadows and felt, as much as saw, the passion that contorted his features and glazed his burning eyes. And then there was nothing but the frantic movement of their bodies as the desperation of their need drove them out of control.

The world erupted in a frenzy of exploding sensations that sent shock waves through her body and penetrated to the deepest corner of her soul. She uttered a long, involuntary cry and heard Walker's rasping "Marty!" and felt his release quake through him.

Their labored breathing was loud in the silence that followed. After long moments, he lifted his head and eased his weight off her. Sinking down beside her, he kissed her and drew her spent body into the shelter of his arms.

Chapter 12

Last week was hell without you." Walker spoke quietly, his cheek resting against the top of her head. They lay in her bed, the sheet and comforter pulled over them.

She ran her hand along his arm, which encircled her waist, then laced their fingers together and rested her arm on his. "It's been bad for me, too."

His heart ached when he thought about the night he'd seen her and Macomber together. He forced back an urge to question her. Why punish himself with the details of that night? Besides, he didn't own her. She'd made that clear.

He smoothed her hair off her brow and kissed it. "That gives me hope."

She was silent for several moments. Then she sighed and said softly, "I could love you, Walker. You must know that."

He wanted to believe that she was already in love with him but was afraid to admit it. His arm tightened around her. "Right now I'll settle for that, honey."

She turned to switch on the bedside lamp and raised herself on one elbow to look down at him. "Have you had dinner?"

He grinned devilishly. "Just dessert, sweetheart."

She laughed. "Umm, and wasn't it delicious?"

"Come here." He pulled her down to kiss her deeply.

His tongue traced her lips and slid inside her mouth. She broke the kiss. "When you kiss me like that, I forget everything else."

His eyes were dark and vulnerable. "That's the idea." He slid his hand over her hip and up to the side of her breast. His thumb stroked the undercurve slowly, and he watched her eyes soften to a deep, liquid gray.

Marty let her heavy lids slide down. How tempting it was to forget the problems between them and lose herself in his lovemaking. She took a deep breath and opened her eyes. She placed her palm against his cheek for a moment, and then she shook herself and sat up. "We have to talk. I'll fix us something to eat." For the first time that day, she felt hungry.

Walker lay on his back, his arms behind his head, watching her as she donned a short, pink nightgown and matching velour robe and scuffs. Tying the robe's belt, she looked at him and smiled. "Don't you want to eat?"

Walker's gaze crept over her tousled blond hair, the high color in her cheeks, her kiss-swollen mouth. He thought she was the most desirable woman he'd ever seen. "Honey, eating is a very weak second on the list of things I'd like to do right now."

She put her hands on her hips and shook her head at him. "To everything there is a season, Walker. Haven't you heard that?"

He gave her a lopsided grin and sat up. "And this is the season for eating," he muttered. "Okay, if you insist. What have you got?"

"How does a chicken sandwich and pumpkin pie sound?"

"Not bad," he admitted.

She left the room. Walker pulled on his socks, jeans and shirt, and joined her in the kitchen. He made coffee while she cut thick slices of homemade whole wheat bread, slathered them with mayonnaise and added lettuce, tomato slices and generous portions of chicken breast.

Walker took a big bite of his sandwich and made a masculine sound of contentment. "I just remembered I haven't eaten since breakfast."

"I thought you might have gone to the Stouts for Thanksgiving dinner."

He looked at her steadily. "They invited me, but I wasn't in a holiday mood. I spent the day at the station so Hemphill could be off. He has a family, and it's a family day. But business was slow, and I had plenty of idle time to think about you. I love you, Marty."

She met his look, her face grave. "I believe you really do, Walker."

"So, where do we go from here?"

"I've done a lot of thinking about our situation this past week. And about me, who and what I am. I've spent most of my life wishing I could change myself." She took a swallow of coffee and made a rueful face. "I'm a psychologist, a person who tries to help other people sort out their feelings and learn to accept and like themselves—what they really are, not just the image somebody else has of them." It was the first time she had put all of this into words, and she spoke slowly, thoughtfully. "Did you know that most of my life I've felt like a failure?"

He shook his head without speaking. He didn't want to interrupt her self-examination.

She continued, "It started when I realized my parents were embarrassed when I told them about my precognitive experiences. They disapproved. Finally, I kept them to myself. But they were a part of me, you see, so what I was doing was withholding myself from other people, denying what my parents convinced me was a serious flaw in me. Denial is a powerful psychological defense."

She ate slowly until only half of her sandwich remained on her plate, and Walker noticed that her cup was empty. Quietly, he rose and poured more coffee. He returned to his chair. She ate more of her sandwich, then lifted her cup and cooled the hot coffee by blowing on it. She swallowed some and set her cup down. "I succeeded pretty well in blocking the experiences from my conscious mind, but they surfaced in dreams. Danny was the first man I was ever serious about, and I knew I had to tell him about my psychic ability before we were married. I put it off until a month before the wedding date. I thought the more time we spent together, and the better he knew me, the easier it would be for him to accept what I had to tell him." She fell silent, her face turned half away from Walker. She was gazing at the blackness beyond the kitchen window.

Walker cleared his throat. "He didn't understand."

She looked back at him. "It wasn't only that it was foreign to his experience. It was outside the realm of what he saw as reality." Walker nodded encouragingly, and she went on. "You'd think I might have learned something by then, but when Danny left I reacted in the same old way." She smiled briefly. "I enrolled in masters' courses and learned all about behavior modification techniques, but I never applied them to myself."

"Like the cobbler who has no shoes?"

"Yes," she agreed. "I simply refused to deal with my precognition. Then I dreamed about Julia Allman, and I had to try to help her." Sadness crept into her eyes. "I'd give anything if I were able to. But one thing the dreams about Julia have made me realize is that I no longer want to change myself. I wouldn't even if I could. I have ESP, and I won't deny it any longer. That doesn't mean I'm going to take out ads and broadcast it, but it's a part of me that I accept."

She ate the rest of her sandwich, and the silence in the kitchen was oppressive. Walker waited, knowing that she hadn't yet said what she'd been working up to. She finally looked at him, and Walker smiled.

"Now you're going to tell me the point of all this."

"Yes." She toyed with the handle of her coffee cup, and Walker could see it wasn't easy for her. She dropped her hand to her lap and took a long breath. "I can't make a commitment to a man who can't deal with every part of me."

Walker chose his words carefully. "You think I can't?"

She was very still. "Be honest with yourself, Walker. What if the story of my pyschic dreams about the Allman girl should become common knowledge, be told in the newspaper. Would it embarrass you?"

He shook his head. "No," he said emphatically. Then he frowned. "I might feel a little uncomfortable if somebody made a joke about it, but that would be because I don't want people laughing at you." His eyes on her face were grave. "I want to marry you, Marty. I know your shocking secret and it doesn't make any difference."

She didn't smile. "But you're still reserving judgment."

He didn't deny it.

"Let's give it some more time." She picked up their plates and carried them to the sink. She cut two big slabs of pumpkin pie and scooped whipped cream on top. We're exactly where we were a week ago, Marty thought, except that I'm no longer trying to make myself believe I can forget him.

Walker ate his pie, knowing that if he tried to pressure her, she would back away from him again. At least she was talking to him. He finished his pie and leaned back in his chair. "It was snowing pretty hard when I got here. The streets are slick as glass."

She propped her chin on the heel of her hand and looked at him, amusement sparkling in her eyes. "I can't turn you out in a blizzard. I guess you'll have to spend the night."

His slow smile made her heart catch in her throat. He came around the table and pulled her to her feet. Hugging her to him, he enveloped her in comforting warmth.

"I can learn to be patient, honey. I won't even ask you not to see other men."

She tilted her head back, her expression perplexed. "There's no other man I want to see."

He contemplated letting it drop there, but he wanted complete honesty between them as much as she did. "I drove by here Tuesday night. I really wasn't trying to spy on you." He bent his head and rested his forehead against hers. "Oh, damn, maybe I was. I saw you going into the house with Macomber. You looked pretty cozy."

She cradled his head between her hands and kissed him. "You're jealous."

"Hell, yes."

She laughed, sounding delighted. "Did you know that jealousy is often an indication of a person's need to control a relationship?"

"Don't talk like a psychologist," he growled.

She relented. "There's absolutely no reason for you to be jealous."

His auburn brows rose in disagreement. "Macomber had his arm around you, and it looked to me like you were kissing him."

"He didn't come inside with me. I kissed his cheek and thanked him for being a good friend. He put his arm around me because he felt sorry for me—himself, too. He'd dressed up and bought me an expensive dinner. We went to the Silver Spoon. There was a small band playing romantic songs, and every one of them reminded me of you. I got all weepy—the evening was a disaster."

Walker grinned and crushed her against him. His mouth staked claim to hers with a hot, moist hunger. After long moments, he muttered, "Thank God," against her lips. "All I could think about was him making love to you."

She looked deeply into his eyes. "I wouldn't have let him, even if he'd tried. You've ruined me for any other man."

He gave a deep, guttural laugh and lifted her into his arms and started toward the bedroom. "I'm going to make sure you stay ruined, love."

Marty recognized the white cabinets and the red-brick linoleum. Her head turned back and forth on the pillow and she began to tremble in her sleep. She saw the calendar for November next to the sink, the table and chairs, the range and refrigerator. Her body tensed because she knew what was coming next. The door next to the refrigerator flew open, and Julia Allman ran into the room. She looked around frantically, her mouth working. But, as in the other dreams,

Marty couldn't make out what Julia was saying. There was no sound. The door was swinging closed, and then it banged open again. The dark-haired man lunged for Julia, and his hands closed around her throat.

Marty whimpered and her eyelids fluttered. She wanted to shout at the man to stop, but she couldn't make a sound.

Suddenly Julia wrenched free of the man's grasp and stumbled back a few steps, gasping for breath. The table was between Julia and the man now. Julia pulled a chair from the table and sent it skidding across the linoleum as she raced back through the door, the way she had come. She was running through another room containing a larger table than the one in the kitchen and several chairs. A dining room. Julia stormed into the living room. It was furnished with a worn brown sofa and a couple of upholstered chairs so dingy it was hard to tell what their original color had been. On the floor, next to the wall, were barbells and a stack of weight plates of graduated sizes. Julia was fumbling with the lock on the front door, looking back over her shoulder, her fingers working frantically.

Marty's heart was racing. She stirred in the bed and, again, tried unsuccessfully to scream.

The dark-haired man suddenly loomed behind Julia and at the same moment she managed to free the lock. She gripped the doorknob, wrenched open the door, and threw herself out of the house. She was now on a wide front porch, and she stumbled down the steps. The man was right behind her, and he caught her in the yard. He was behind her with his arm around her throat, cutting off her air. He was trying to drag her back to the house.

Marty shot upright in bed. "No! Let her go!" She was breathing hard and her heart was as loud as a hammer in her ears.

Walker struggled from the depths of sleep. Marty was sitting up; he could feel her shaking. "Shh, sweetheart. It's only a dream." He put his arms around her and pulled her down beside him. Marty was still gulping air and whimpering. "Shh, it's all right. I'm here."

Marty clung to him, seeking the comfort and reassurance of his warm, strong body. She shuddered and her arms tightened around his neck. He stroked her back and kissed her forehead. "Bad dream, huh?"

"I saw Julia and that man again."

He continued to stroke her. "Same as before?"

"Yes, but there was more this time. She got away from him in the kitchen and ran through the house. She made it as far as the front yard before he caught her." She shivered. "It was night."

She was silent for several moments, and Walker wondered if she'd gone back to sleep. Then she said, "Checking health clubs was a waste of time. He has weight equipment in his living room."

Walker felt a nervous tremor run through him. "You think Julia's still alive?"

"Yes." She drew in an unsteady breath and began to cry silently. Finally she choked out, "I don't know why he's kept her alive this long, but he's going to kill her soon. Oh, Walker, I feel so responsible for that poor girl."

"You're not responsible, sweetheart."

"But I'm the only one who really believes she's still alive."

"That's not true. We haven't found any evidence that she's dead. The investigation is proceeding on the assumption that she's alive." He fell into a thoughtful silence, his hand still stroking her absently. She stopped weeping and wiped her eyes with a corner of the sheet. "Did you see anything else?" Walker asked.

She let her mind go back to the dream, recalling it from the beginning. She saw Julia break free in the kitchen, push a chair in her kidnapper's path, race through the dining room and living room, fumble with the lock, throw open the door, run out on the porch and then into the yard. Light spilled from the house through the open front door, revealing a weathered wood porch, a bit of wall siding—asbestos perhaps—and ... Marty gasped, "I saw part of the house number beside the front door—the last two numbers..." She closed her eyes and tried to bring the numbers back. "One-eight," she said finally, "eighteen." She lifted her head from Walker's shoulder, excited. "Maybe you can find him from that. How many houses could there be in Willow with the last numbers one-eight?"

"Quite a few, I expect. You're sure now the house is in Willow?"

She hesitated, then lay back down. "No."

"I'll file a report," Walker said, settling her more comfortably against him. "Don't worry yourself sick over something you can't help. Try to get some sleep now."

But it was a long time before she slept. She listened to Walker's deep, even breathing against the background of the wailing wind, and replayed the dream in her mind again and again. She concentrated on the end of the dream, trying to "see" more of the house number. But the numerals flashed briefly and the light was too dim to catch more than the last two.

She tried not to be angry with Walker for his response. He'd file a report, he'd said. It wasn't quite as bad as patting her on the head and saying, "there, there," but it was close. Obviously he still had no confidence in her dreams. The report would be stuck in the file and forgotten.

Regardless of what Walker said, she still felt responsible. She *knew* Julia was alive; the police were merely proceeding "on the assumption" that she was. Somehow she felt their approach lacked the sense of urgency that prodded her.

She would have to follow up on her own; it was the only thing she could do and still live with herself. She remembered the terror that had filled her when she faced William Welch alone. A confrontation like that with the real killer would be far more dangerous. Just thinking about it frightened her. She would have to be more careful this time.

Walker went to Jess's office as soon as the chief arrived. He closed the door behind him and said, "Marty had another dream about Julia Allman."

Jess was hanging his overcoat on a rack in the corner. His expression changed instantly from depression to alertness. He went to his desk and sat down, motioning Walker to take the other chair. "Like the others?" Walker could tell he was trying not to get his hopes up.

"It was the same up to a point, but this one lasted longer. She saw Julia get away from the kidnapper in the kitchen then run through the house and go out the front door. He caught her there. But the interesting thing is Marty saw part of the house number. She says the last two numerals are one-eight."

Jess pursed his lips in thought. "This could be the clue we've been waiting for."

Walker nodded. "Or it could be nothing."

Jess scrutinized Walker's face. "Still don't believe her, do you?" Walker shrugged. "But I take it you're seeing her again. This is the first morning in a week that you haven't looked like you were in the last stages of a terminal illness."

"Yes, I'm seeing her. I got a reprieve." His lips curved in a half smile. "And I didn't lie to her. I still have doubts. I don't know whether Marty's dreams are true precognition or not, Jess, but she is utterly convinced they are. I love her, so I guess it's time to trust her—at least, until I have more evidence, one way or the other."

Jess frowned. "She was wrong about Welch."

Walker nodded. "Now she says that checking health clubs was a mistake because the guy we want works out at home. She saw weight equipment in her dream."

Jess thought for a moment, then heaved a sigh. "The newspaper editor is after our tails. Did you read the editorial yesterday?"

"Yeah." The editor had called for evidence of progress in the case or Jess's resignation. He pleaded with the citizens of Willow to get on their telephones to their city councilmen and demand action. He closed with the suggestion that an "experienced investigator" be brought in to direct the inquiry. "Happy Thanksgiving," Walker commented sourly.

"We got nothing to lose. What do you want to do?"

"I want to follow up on the house number."

"How many men do you need?"

"Let's keep this thing under wraps. If nobody knows about it and it turns out to be a wild-goose chase, they won't have more ammunition to use against us."

Jess snorted. "Doesn't appear to me that they need any more."

"I don't even want Marty to know. She'd be devastated if it ended up being another mistake. We're just lucky the paper didn't get hold of that."

Jess made a gesture of agreement. "Hemphill can keep his lip buttoned." He grunted. "Of course, you'll have to put up with his jokes."

Walker nodded. "That's who I had in mind. Maybe his jokes will take my mind off our troubles." He made a doleful sound. "For a minute or two. I'll lay it out for him and swear him to secrecy. We can start immediately if the other duty officers can handle everything else."

"I'll fix it. May have to pay some overtime." Jess pondered that. "Well, look at it this way. If this pans out, the council will be so happy they won't care about the overtime. If it doesn't, I'm not gonna be around to take the flack."

Walker stood and went to the door. "I better catch Hemphill before he goes out on patrol."

"Walker." Jess sounded suddenly dubious. But all he said was, "Use discretion, and be careful."

A few minutes later Walker and Hemphill were in Walker's police car, headed for Walker's house. Walker had explained the detail to Hemphill, who didn't try to hide his surprise that Jess and Walker meant to investigate something seen in a dream. "You got a better suggestion?" Walker asked him, and Hemphill had to admit that he didn't. "We'll take my car," Walker went on. "We don't want to draw any more attention to ourselves than we have to."

"So, what do we do besides look for houses that have one-eight in the address?"

"We have to get inside."

"That shouldn't be hard. Most people want to co-operate with the law."

"All except the guy we're looking for."

"Well, we can worry about that when the time comes."

"We'll ask for a drink of water. I have to see the kitchen before I'll be sure enough to go any further."

Walker had already told Hemphill about the kitchen Marty had described. Now Hemphill looked at Walker and shook his head in disbelief. "I never thought I'd see the day when you and Jess would bring a psychic in on a case."

"We didn't bring her in," Walker said shortly. "She came to us."

His defensive tone was not lost on Hemphill. Nelda had told him Walker was dating this Newland woman. He seemed pretty serious about the whole thing. Better be careful what he said to Walker, because lately just about everything made him snappy. Best to change the subject. "Hey!" Hemphill slapped his leg. "Did I ever tell you the one about the girdle salesman and the farmer's daughter?"

Chapter 13

Officially the clinic was closed the day after Thanksgiving, but Marty had fallen behind in her patient records and she spent the day working. The previous night's two-inch snowfall had glazed the streets, and most people were staying inside. With only an occasional car passing by and the clinic door locked, Marty's office provided the undisturbed quiet she needed to bring her files up to date.

Just before noon, she heard a key in the lock of the outer door, then the loud stamping of feet.

"Marty?"

She recognized Jerry's voice and went out to the reception room. Jerry was sitting in a chair, tugging off rubber boots. He'd already removed his topcoat and set the wet boots on the mat next to the door. "I rec-

ognized your car. What are you doing here on a holiday?''

"Catching up on some office work. What's your
excuse?"

He made a face. "The same. Teaching that class at
the college has thrown me behind here."

"The phone hasn't rung once since I arrived. I've
been able to get a lot done."

He looked at her quizzically. "You're all bright-eyed
and bushy-tailed today. Have a nice Thanksgiving?"

"Uh-huh."

His eyes narrowed as he feigned deep thought. He
stroked an imaginary beard. "I see-ee. Dr. Macomber will now make a brilliant deduction. You are
seeing the gallant Officer Dietrick again."

Marty laughed. "How did you know?"

"Elementary, my dear. You look rested for the first
time in a week. I was starting to worry about you."

Jerry was right. Except for being wakened by the
dream, she had slept well last night. Walker had
roused her at eight with coffee and a kiss just before
he left for the station. "Ah, that's sweet of you, Jer.
But as you can see, there's no need."

He leaned back against the vinyl covered chair and
stretched, his arms extended. "So," he said, letting his
arms drop, "the man finally came to his senses and
realized he'd been an idiot to let you get away. I take
it everything is hunky-dory now."

Marty cocked her head. "We still have a few problems to work out, but things are more hunky-dory
than they were last Tuesday night. I still feel bad when

I remember how I spoiled your evening. By the way, Walker drove by the house as you were bringing me home. He assumed the worst." She smiled, remembering Walker's jealousy.

Jerry sat on the edge of his chair. "I hope you set him straight. I would not like to have Officer Dietrick on my case. I abhor violence, especially when the other guy is bigger than I am."

"Not to worry," Marty soothed. "I told him we're just friends."

He slumped back against the chair. "Thank God."

She chuckled. "I thought you were going to Wichita to see your folks."

"I had a change in plans." He looked smug. "I met this woman Wednesday night. Actually, she's a friend of a buddy of mine's fiancée. Her name's Heather. She's a nurse at the hospital." He looked abstracted for a moment. "Big brown eyes and the pertest little derriere you ever saw. I think I'm in love."

"Again?"

"Umm." He seemed to shake himself out of a daydream. "She was off yesterday, but had to work today. Her family lives in Minnesota, and she was going to be alone on Thanksgiving. Being a true gentleman, I obviously couldn't drive off to Wichita and leave poor Heather to eat her turkey and cranberry sauce alone."

"Obviously," Marty said dryly. "How did your parents take the change in plans?"

"They didn't threaten to disinherit me or anything like that. They were really pretty sporting about it. The whole clan was expected—my two brothers and three sisters and assorted in-laws and out-laws. With all the hullabaloo, they probably didn't miss me much. Except they didn't have anyone to gang up on."

Marty looked puzzled.

"I'm the only one who isn't married," Jerry explained. "You wouldn't believe the women they've trotted out for my inspection. I haven't figured out if they really think I'd be happier married, or if it's just a case of misery loving company."

"You're impossible," Marty told him. "Does Heather know how you feel about domesticity?"

He flashed a big grin. "It's not going to be a problem. Heather's twenty-six and doesn't want to settle down for years yet."

"She told you that?"

"Yep."

Marty shook her head. "Jer, you're such an innocent."

"You don't think she means it?"

Marty smiled and shrugged.

"You don't know her. She's—well, she's different."

"You're probably right," Marty said, but her eyes still twinkled. "I made a pot of coffee. I'm going back to work. There's something important I have to do later."

Jerry rose and ambled to the small pantry off the reception room, where the coffeepot was. "With Dietrick?" he chortled over his shoulder.

"No, I have to do this alone."

Jerry got his coffee and followed Marty to her office. Leaning against the door frame, he said, "Sounds mysterious."

"It's private," Marty said.

Jerry looked disappointed. "Okay, okay, I can take a hint." He went to his office and closed the door.

Marty went back to her files, aware each time she wrote the date—November twenty-fifth—that there were only five days left in the month. The knowledge spurred her to finish quickly. At three-thirty she said goodbye to Jerry and left the clinic. She drove cautiously on the slick streets to the west edge of Willow. The car threatened to go into a slide twice, but she was traveling slowly enough to correct it. Fortunately there still wasn't much traffic. She decided to forget the newer housing additions west of town and look for houses whose numbers ended in one-eight on the older residential streets.

She hadn't expected there to be so many of them. Unfortunately, most of them had frame exteriors and front porches. After driving by ten such houses, she was confused and discouraged. The house in her dream could be any one—or none—of them. By that time it was getting dark, and although she could still read most of the numbers, she was tense from navigating the icy streets. Her shoulders ached and she was hungry. Walker had promised to be at her house at seven with a pizza. She drove home.

While Walker worked the evening shift Saturday, Marty resumed her slow journey through Willow.

Sometimes it was necessary to check the street curb with her flashlight to be sure of the address. She tried to fight off a growing feeling of hopelessness, but it wasn't easy. All the houses were starting to look alike, and she had no strong feeling about any of them. But she kept going because it was the only thing she could think of to do.

About seven-thirty, she turned onto Juniper Street. It was getting too dark; she might as well go home. She'd check a few more blocks, and then give it up for tonight.

She slowed the car to a crawl as it crossed an inter-secting street. If the addresses on Juniper ran parallel with those on the street she'd just left, there should be a house numbered 2618 midway in this block. She stopped in front of a weathered two-story house. There was no yard light so she couldn't read the number on the house. Wrapping her gray cashmere scarf around her head, she grabbed the flashlight and got out. She walked to the front of the car and she shone the light on the curb. There it was, 2618. Hurrying back to the comparative warmth of the car, she locked the door and gazed at the shadowy outlines of the house. Could this be the one? She stared at the house until her eyes felt dry and uncomfortable.

With a sigh, she put her head back against the seat. What was the use? This crazy driving up and down streets was accomplishing nothing. She closed her eyes to ease the dryness. She'd finish on Juniper Street and go home.

She heard the sound of a car engine. She opened her eyes and blinked as headlights reflected blindingly in her rearview mirror. A car was pulling up to the curb behind her. Oh, no, she couldn't handle another indignant homeowner like Welch! The headlights behind her went out. A surge of adrenaline pumped into her blood; all she could think of was getting away. Her fingers closed over the key in the ignition.

There was a muffled thumping of gloved knuckles against the passenger window. "Marty! Open up!"

She jerked her hand away from the key, leaned across the seat and opened the door. "Walker!"

He got in, bringing a rush of cold air with him, and slammed the door. He leaned toward her, his right hand on the dash, his left arm resting on the back of the seat. "What are you doing?"

He was clearly upset. Where had he come from? He was supposed to be working. "Are you following me?"

"No. I just happened to be in the neighborhood."

She cupped her gloved hand over her cold nose and blew to warm it. She didn't know whether to believe him or not. Well, if he could be evasive, she could, too. "So did I."

His hand snaked along the back of the seat and curved around the side of her neck. Under other circumstances, she would have felt a tingle of excitement at his touch. But his features were set and grim; he was definitely not in a romantic mood. "I see, and you just happened to stop in front of 2618, right?"

It took a moment for his words to sink in. "How did you know the address?" He looked at her steadily without answering, and her eyes widened. "You're here for the same reason I am, aren't you?"

"You haven't yet told me what your reason is," he pointed out.

Her cold lips curved in a dazzling grin. "Walker Dietrick, you know I'm looking for the house I saw in my dream!" There was a faint softening of his jawline. She added accusingly, "And so are you!" She threw her arms around his neck and hugged him, nuzzling her cold nose into the warm scarf at his neck.

After a moment's hesitation, his arms closed around her, and she felt him relax. "You need a keeper to make sure you stay out of trouble," he muttered, turning his face into her silky hair.

All at once, discouragement overwhelmed her. "Oh, Walker, it seems so hopeless. I must have looked at twenty houses, but I don't feel anything." Neither of them spoke for a while. Walker pulled her closer and she snuggled against his warmth. Finally she lifted her head to look at him. "You *have* been checking houses with numbers ending in one-eight, haven't you?"

He nodded and kissed the cold tip of her nose. "Yes, we have."

She frowned. "I don't see how you hope to find Julia this way. I'm not sure *I* would recognize the house, but you haven't even seen it."

"I think I'd know the kitchen if I saw it."

She felt a sudden elation. "You've been going in-side...? And who's 'we'?"

"Hemphill and I. Jess put us on this full time. We started out together, but realized it was going to take days and split up. He's working an area on the east side right now. We knock on a door and say we're looking for a robbery suspect who was reported seen in the neighborhood. We say we'd like to come in and ask a few questions. Once we get inside, we ask for a drink. Then we follow the resident to the kitchen. Of course, some people aren't at home, so we have to keep retracing our steps. We've seen about thirty-five kitchens so far, including this one." He gestured with his thumb toward the house in front of which they were parked. He hated to sound so pessimistic, but he had to. "We haven't found one like the kitchen in your dream—so far."

She looked momentarily saddened, but brightened again. "But you're looking. You believe me. Oh, Walker, thank you."

She offered her mouth for his kiss, and he was happy to accept the invitation. Some moments later, he lifted his head and laughed a little unsteadily. "If we keep this up, I'll forget I'm on duty." He smiled as she reluctantly opened her eyes. He enclosed the tip of her nose tightly in his gloved fingers. "Your nose is cold."

"So are my feet."

"You should be at home. Hemphill and I will han-dle this detail. We decided to work evenings because we can find more people at home then."

She gazed at him solemnly. "Do you know what day it is, Walker?"

"Yeah, the twenty-sixth."

"That means you have four days—at the most."

"Honey, let us worry about that."

She shook her head abruptly. "It's possible that you might not recognize the kitchen. You haven't seen it, Walker—but I have."

He looked very stern, all at once. "What are you suggesting?"

"I want to go with you."

She could see him marshaling his arguments. "This guy is nuts, Marty. I don't want you anywhere near him."

"Julia has been his prisoner for more than a month." She let that linger between them for a moment, then went on. "I won't say a word, I promise. Just take me with you and let me see inside the houses." He was already shaking his head. She rushed on, "If you don't, Walker, I swear I'll keep looking on my own."

He gazed at her despairingly. "If Jess finds out I've involved a civilian..."

"I'm not just any civilian. I have knowledge that can help you."

His shoulders seemed to sag. "Okay, Marty, but only because I know you're stubborn enough to go on by yourself. It seems to be the best way to keep you out of trouble. But, remember, I do all the talking." He shook his head. "Dammit, if we do find that guy and you're with me..."

"I won't give it away," she said and hugged him again.

It was Monday evening, November twenty-eighth. After taking a thirty-minute break for dinner, Marty and Walker left a Main Street restaurant to resume their slow and so-far fruitless checking of houses. Temperatures had been in the forties during the day. Most of the snow and ice had melted and the streets were dry. They were making better time than they had the evening before.

"We should meet Hemphill somewhere on College Avenue in about two hours," Walker said as he opened the car door for Marty. "By then we'll have covered most of the addresses ending in one-eight in Willow, except for the new houses west of town."

When he got into the driver's seat, she said, "Don't forget the ones where no one was home. We haven't checked back on all those yet."

He drove away from the restaurant. "Yeah." He reached for her hand and squeezed it through two layers of glove. She knew he was trying not to give up hope, but his manner all evening had been discouraged. "Marty," he said tentatively, "if we don't find her, we have to remember that we did everything we could." Now he was trying to prepare her to face failure.

"Don't even think it!" She leaned closer to the windshield and began reading street signs. "That's Holly Street just ahead."

They stopped in front of 118 South Holly. The house was covered with asbestos siding that had probably been white twenty or thirty years ago. What could be seen of the siding now in the deepening dusk appeared gray, and several pieces had broken off, exposing the dark wood beneath. But the house was in no worse shape than most of its neighbors; the people who lived in this part of town were low on the socio-economic scale. There was an old pickup truck parked in the graveled driveway.

"There's a light at the back of the house," Walker said. "Looks like somebody's home." He reached out and pulled the wide collar of Marty's jacket higher to cover her ears. The wind wasn't bad, but the temperature had dropped below freezing again. "Are you sure you don't want to wait for me here?"

"I want to go."

His big hand rested at the side of her head for a moment. "Okay, let's do it."

There was no front walk. The soggy ground squished underfoot as they crossed the yard. They climbed three wide steps to reach the porch. Walker opened the sagging screen door and rapped on the inner door.

To Marty the sound seemed oddly ominous. A quiver ran through her. She plunged her hands into the deep pockets of her jacket and shuffled her booted feet to ward off the numbing effect of the cold. She heard heavy footsteps inside the house.

The door opened a crack. "What do you want?" It was a man's voice.

Walker thrust his open wallet, with his *ID* showing, up to the crack. "I'm Officer Dietrick with the Willow Police Department, sir. There's been a robbery in the next block. The burglar got away, but we think he's still in the neighborhood. I'd like to ask you some questions."

The man on the other side of the door was silent for a moment. The crack did not widen. "I haven't been out all day. I don't know anything about a robbery."

"I'm supposed to question everybody in this block." Walker sounded like a humble good-old-boy, worried about what his chief would say if he didn't carry out instructions to the letter. "I'll only take a few minutes of your time."

Silence. Then the door opened slowly. "Who's she?"

"This is Rookie Newland," Walker said, not looking at Marty, who followed him into the house. "I'm showing her the ropes." He gave the black-haired man a friendly grin. "I didn't catch your name, sir."

"Robert Danvers," the man mumbled, his gaze falling to Walker's holstered gun. He wasn't as tall as Walker, but he was broader. The bulges of big shoulders and arms could be seen beneath his long-sleeved knit shirt. He stood with his feet spread and his thumb hooked over the back pockets of his jeans. His manner was resentful, almost belligerent.

The house had an aura that slammed Marty in the face the moment she stepped inside. She still stood just inside the front door, and it was an effort not to clutch her throat because she felt suddenly as though she couldn't get enough oxygen. She had started to shake. To hide it, she braced herself against the closed door and kept her hands stuffed in her pockets and her eyes lowered. She was afraid to look around the room, afraid that her eyes would give away the rigid fear that had gripped her.

"What you wanta ask me?" Danvers said. "I don't have much time."

Walker took his time getting his notepad and pen from the pocket of his leather jacket. He flipped the pad open. "I could sure use a drink of water, Mr. Danvers, if you don't mind."

Danvers muttered something under his breath and walked out of the room. Walker followed. Marty's feet felt as though they were weighted. She stayed where she was because the thought of going further into the house frightened her. There was evil here. Danvers crossed the dining room and went through a door into what was evidently the kitchen. Walker followed. As soon as they were out of sight, Marty forced herself to step deeper into the living room and make a quick survey. The only light was from the dining room, but she could see well enough to identify the sofa and two dingy armchairs she had seen in her dream. Her gaze darted to the west wall. Barbells lay against the baseboard with extra weight plates stacked next to them. For an instant, she couldn't pull her eyes away. Her mind seemed caught in the same grip of terror that had clutched her body. She was shaking so hard that she had to clench her jaw to keep her teeth from chattering.

She heard Walker and Danvers talking in the kitchen. Walker was carrying on his fake investigation and Danvers was answering in short monosyllables. Marty couldn't make herself go back there and open the door. But she didn't need to know what the kitchen looked like.

Julia Allman was here. She could feel it. She strained to hear, but except for the two male voices from the kitchen, there was no other sound. Marty could see an opening in the east wall of the dining room. It led to what appeared to be a hall. There would be a bathroom and bedrooms off the hall. Did he have Julia imprisoned in one of them? She was trying to pump up enough courage to go and look when the kitchen door opened and Walker and Danvers came out.

Walker was tucking his pen and notepad into a jacket pocket. "Thank you for your cooperation, Mr. Danvers," he said enthusiastically. "If you should see anyone in the neighborhood acting suspicious, I'd appreciate if you'd call the station and let us know." Walker came toward Marty, who had resumed her frozen position near the front door. "Come on, Newland. We'll go back to the station and I'll show you how to write up the report."

"Walker—" Marty's throat was so tight, her lips so stiff, that her voice sounded strange.

Walker gripped her arm and opened the door. "Thanks again, Mr. Danvers. Come on, Newland, get a move on." Marty's legs refused to work properly. Walker practically lifted her out onto the porch. Then he put his arm around her waist and hurried her down the steps.

He could feel her shaking. He didn't slow his pace, which was just short of a run. "Keep walking," he said under his breath. "Don't look back."

The fear in Marty's throat tasted like iron. As she realized they were going back to the car, she grew frantic. They were walking away from Julia!

"He's the one," she forced out.

Walker's steps didn't falter. "I know." He opened the passenger door and urged her inside, then loped around the car and got in. He started the engine and reached for his radio speaker.

"Why didn't you arrest him?" Marty wailed.

Walker drove away from the house, talking into the speaker, requesting backup from Hemphill and whoever else could get to the address quickly. He turned the corner and parked out of sight of Danvers's house.

"Walker, Julia's in there! I can feel it!"

He reached for her and ran his hands along her arms to comfort her. "Calm down, honey. I'm going in there as soon as my backup arrives. I couldn't risk taking him alone, not with you there. For all we know, he could have confederates with him. They could take Julia out the back while I'm trying to deal with Danvers."

Oh, God, she hadn't thought of that. The radio crackled and a voice asked for directions to Walker. Walker kept one arm around Marty. One-eighteen South Holly, Phillips," he said. "No sirens—and turn your lights out when you turn the corner." He replaced the speaker and wrapped both arms around Marty again. "It's incredible, sweetheart," he said. "The kitchen was exactly like you described it. White cabinets, red-brick linoleum, table and chairs in the center of the room, even the calendar next to the sink."

Marty felt no sense of vindication. She thought about Julia in there with Danvers and shivered.

"I'm sorry I ever doubted you, honey."

At that moment there was no pleasure in hearing the words. "Walker, he's going to kill her tonight—any minute." The certainty was stronger than any hunch she'd ever had.

Walker opened the car door. "I'm going back up the street to wait for Hemphill and Phillips."

Marty scrambled out of the car. "I can't stay here by myself. I'll go crazy."

He took her hand and they crept across yards back toward 118 South Holly, keeping to the inky shadows next to the houses. They halted beside a holly hedge next door to 118. "Walker," Marty whispered urgently, "look, there's a light on in the basement. That must be where he has Julia."

Walker tugged on her arm. "Get down!" He released his gun from the holster and drew it out. Two cars with their lights out approached from the north end of the street. "There's my backup. Stay here, Marty. There could be gunfire."

"Walker, be careful . . . I love you!" But he was already gone, crouched over, running toward the two cars that had stopped down the street.

Hunkered down and peering through an opening in the hedge, Marty saw two dark forms get out of the cars and join Walker at the corner of Danvers's yard. They huddled together, whispering urgently. Then they separated, one running stealthily toward the back of the house. Walker and a second officer approached the house from opposite corners of the front yard.

Marty put her hands over her mouth to keep from crying out to Walker again to be careful. She prayed.

He watched from the dark living room until he saw the police car drive away. Alarm energized him, and he paced. The urge to bolt from the house and run through the cold night was on him again, but he controlled himself. He had to think about what to do.

It was possible the officer had been investigating a burglary, just as he'd said. But he didn't trust the police. He particularly didn't trust Dietrick, who had seemed too friendly, as though Dietrick had wanted to put him off his guard.

His lip curled as he remembered the big, red-haired cop's questions. Had he noticed a stranger in the neighborhood? Had he seen anyone running or driving fast down the street earlier that evening? He'd told Dietrick that he had neither seen nor heard anything unusual. Dietrick had written it all down in his little notebook. Stupid cop. But something told him Dietrick wasn't as naive as he'd acted.

He prowled through the house, cursing, breathing rapidly. Things had been going wrong for a week, and that cop showing up on his doorstep was another warning signal.

The girl in the basement was not Rita. He'd been fighting it all week, but there were too many gestures that were wrong, too many things she "couldn't remember" about their childhood. She didn't even look as much like Rita as he had thought at first.

She was clever, though. After the first few days, when she was still saying that Julia Allman was her real name, she'd changed her mind and sworn she was Rita. She'd almost made him believe it. He hadn't slept at all last night. He'd lain awake, trying to decide what to do about her. During the time she had been here with him, he'd come to admire her. She had strength, and at times he almost found himself loving her. He hadn't wanted to admit that she was lying to him. He had wanted to give himself more time to be sure.

Then the cop had knocked at his door and he'd opened it. Weird how that was the moment when he'd finally been certain that the girl in the basement was Julia Allman, just like the newspaper said, and not Rita. In that moment he'd felt weary beyond belief, knowing his search wasn't finished, that he'd made another mistake. He had to start all over again. She was a heartless liar, like his mother.

He had to kill her, of course.

But not here. What if Dietrick decided to come back?

An uncontrollable need to make haste came over him. This was all her fault! He could have been out looking for Rita for weeks, but she'd lulled him into false hope with her lies.

He went to his closet, took his padded down jacket from its hanger and put it on. He noticed the white silk scarf on another hanger and reached for it. He stroked the silk lovingly for a moment, his eyes glittering with anticipation. He'd tie it around her pretty neck and pull it tighter and tighter...

He stuffed the scarf in his pocket, strode back to the hall and unlocked the door to the basement stairs. He clambered down. He noticed that his hand was shaking when he unlocked the lower door. Rage was building in him. He had to get her away from here before it exploded.

She was lying on the cot. "Get up!" he snarled.

She obeyed, his angry tone alerting and frightening her. "What's wrong?"

She was wearing jeans, a cotton shirt, and the brown loafers she'd been wearing when he abducted her from the college campus. He grabbed her sweater and threw it at her. "Put this on. We're going out."

She thrust her arms into the sweater and he jerked her toward the door and pushed her up the stairs ahead of him.

He shouldn't have let her see he was angry. When she reached the landing, she gave a sudden wrench and twisted away from him. She sprinted down the hall, and he stormed after her. She reached the dining room and threw herself through the kitchen door without slackening her pace. She was yelling, "Help! Somebody help me!" He ran after her and caught her near the sink.

Before he knew what he was doing, his hands closed about her throat. "Shut up, liar! Liar! You're not Rita!" He was almost sobbing the words, beside himself with rage and frustration. She was choking and struggling desperately to get away. God, it felt good to have his hands on her throat. She had deceived him. She deserved to die!

A red haze clouded his eyes. He felt her go limp, and he blinked to clear his vision. Her face was white, her eyes closed. He stared at his hands as the rage in him ebbed a little. What was he doing? He didn't want to kill her here. He had to control himself until they were miles away. He loosened his grip.

She came to life instantly; she'd been playing possum. He'd forgotten how clever she was. Gasping to draw air into her oxygen-starved lungs, she leaped around the table, grabbed the top of a chair and spun it across the floor in front of him, then raced back through the door and into the dining room. He grabbed the chair, lifted it from the floor and threw it out of his way. By the time he reached the dining room, she was fumbling at the front door.

He hadn't locked it after the cop left!

He sprinted into the living room and lunged toward her, his hands outstretched. Before he could reach her, she got the door open and ran outside. He followed, half-running and half-falling down the steps behind her. He got a good hold on her finally.

She started screaming again. "Help! Help!"

He got behind her and bent his arm beneath her chin. He pressed against her windpipe and cut off her air. He was amazed at how much strength there could be in such a small body. He couldn't risk taking her somewhere else. She might get away again. He started dragging her back toward the house. She was scratching his arm and trying to kick him.

"You shouldn't have lied to me," he sneered. "Now you have to die, just like the other one."

He got one foot on the bottom step. A deep, menacing voice came out of the darkness.

"Freeze, Danvers!"

He stopped. Before he could assimilate what was happening, a cop he'd never seen before came out of his house through the front door with a gun in his hand.

The voice behind him—he thought it was Dietrick—spoke again. "There are three guns pointed at your head, Danvers. Let her go and reach for the sky. Now!"

Chapter 14

Marty sat in the front seat of Walker's police car, her arms around Julia Allman. The girl wore only a light sweater, and she was trembling uncontrollably. That was probably as much from shock as the below-freezing temperature, Marty thought. She had started the engine and the heater was going full blast.

As soon as Danvers had released Julia, Walker had yelled for Marty to take the girl to the car. Walker and the other officers had subdued Danvers and handcuffed him. They were escorting him to one of the other police cars now.

"You're going to be all right, Julia," Marty soothed. "It's over now."

"Thank God...thank God..." Julia's voice broke and she began to sob wrenchingly.

Marty held her and kept murmuring comforting words. She was glad that Julia was crying. At first the girl had been unable to talk or do anything except lock her muscles against the shaking, as though she were afraid to let go, afraid to feel. Julia's rigid muscles began to relax and she slumped against Marty. Her head rested on Marty's shoulder and the sobs racked her. But tears were preferable to the unnatural control she'd exhibited up to now.

Marty found some tissues in her pocket and handed them to Julia. "That's it, cry all you want to. You'll feel better."

It was some time before the girl's tears stopped. The crying left her limp and swollen-eyed. She moved away from Marty a little and put her head back against the seat. She looked too thin; she'd probably lost weight during her captivity. Her tangled brown hair was pinned away from her face; it needed shampooing. She wasn't shaking anymore.

"Are you warm enough?" Marty asked. The heater was effective; the temperature inside the car must be more than eighty degrees now.

Julia nodded, and Marty turned the heater down to low.

Julia's hands gripped each other in her lap. "He's insane," she said in a low voice.

"I know." Marty placed her hand over Julia's and pressed lightly.

"He was going to kill me."

"Yes. We were afraid he already had." Marty knew she had to ask if Danvers had molested Julia. The girl might need counseling, anyway, but if she'd been raped, it was imperative. "Julia, did he harm you physically?"

She turned her head and looked at Marty. In the light from the dash, Marty could see that her eyes were drawn and dull. It would be some time before Julia was herself again. "Rape, you mean? No, he hardly touched me—except when I tried to get away. He thought I was his sister. At first, I tried to convince him he'd made a mistake. But after I realized he was crazy, that he was the one who had murdered Linda Niles, I decided to play along with him." She frowned. "I finally figured out that his sister—Rita—died when they were young. It was like he needed me to be Rita. When I said I wasn't, he got furious." She shuddered and hugged herself. "There's so much hostility and rage in that man. So to stay alive, I said I was Rita."

"That was smart. It probably saved your life," Marty said.

"He kept me locked in the basement."

"Julia, he can't hurt you anymore."

Her head jerked up abruptly and she grabbed Marty's arm. "I won't have to see him again, will I? I mean, at a trial or anything? I don't think I can handle that."

"There won't be a trial for a long time," Marty assured her, hoping she was right. "He'll be committed to a mental institution for observation and evaluation first. That could take months."

Her hold on Marty's arm slowly relaxed. "The last few days, he'd come down to the basement and just stare at me. It was so scary. After he watched me for a while, he'd ask me questions about his and Rita's childhood. I didn't know the answers, so I said I couldn't remember. Then tonight—'' She closed her eyes and swallowed hard. "Tonight he came downstairs and told me he was taking me out of the house. He said I'd lied to him, that I wasn't Rita. He—he was going to take me somewhere and kill me."

"The police were closing in on him. I went to Danvers's house earlier this evening with Officer Dietrick. We said we were investigating a robbery in the neighborhood to get inside. We left so Walker—Officer Dietrick—could radio for help. Maybe Danvers suspected what was going on. Maybe that's why he was taking you away. It's difficult to know what goes on in a psychotic's mind."

Julia shook her head. "No, he meant to kill me tonight, either in the house or somewhere else. It didn't matter." She studied Marty. "I just realized I don't even know your name."

"Marty Newland."

"Are you a police officer?"

"No, but I've been working with them. It's a long story. I'll tell you about it later, if you want me to."

Walker came to the car then. Marty moved over, and Walker got in. "I'm Walker Dietrick, Julia. Are you all right?"

Julia looked down at her hands and nodded. Walker glanced at Marty and she also nodded. Walker put the car in gear and drove down the street toward the center of town. "Your parents have been notified, Julia. They'll meet you at the station."

She looked over at him. "They're in Willow?"

He nodded. "They've been staying in a motel here ever since you disappeared."

Julia started to cry again, but silently this time. Big tears trickled down her face. Marty put out her hand and Julia grabbed it and hung on. "Will he be there?"

"Danvers?" Walker asked. "The other officers are taking him to the station now. He'll be in a cell. You won't see him."

"Good. I just want to see my parents and go home."

Nobody spoke for a moment. Then Walker said, "I have to ask you some questions, Julia. And we'll want you to sign a statement. I'll make it as fast as I can."

"Okay," she said miserably, and her tears continued.

At the station, Julia ran into her parents' arms. While the Allmans were alternately crying and assuring themselves that Julia was in one piece, Walker asked another officer to drive Marty home. "You were a big help with Julia tonight," he told her, "I'm glad you were there."

"So am I."

"Smith is going to drive you home now. This could take a while. Is it all right if I come by later? It might be very late."

"I'll never forgive you if you don't."

He smiled and bent his head for a quick kiss, not caring who was watching.

Jess came through the front door of the station at that moment and stopped in his tracks. As Marty passed him, he put out his hand to stop her. "If not for you, Marty, we wouldn't have got to her in time. Thank you doesn't seem enough to say."

"It's more than enough, Jess. I'm glad it's over."

He patted her arm and went over to Walker and clapped him on the back. "Good work, Walker. I phoned one of the councilmen before I left home. The whole city council will probably be down here soon and the reporters, too. I'm gonna enjoy telling them how the dedicated officers of the W.P.D. solved the case. With a lot of help from Marty, of course. Do you think she'll mind if I mention that?"

"You'll have to ask her, Jess."

Jess looked at him slyly. "Nice show you and she were putting on when I came in."

Walker nodded, smiling.

"Yep." Jess clapped his back again. "Some woman, that Marty. Smart. Pretty. You better keep an eye on her or somebody's liable to take her away from you."

"It'll never happen."

"Oh, yeah? Damned sure of yourself, aren't you?"

"Not so much sure as determined. I'm going to marry her, Jess."

It was after midnight when Walker knocked at Marty's door. As soon as Officer Smith had brought her home, she'd showered and put on a gown and robe. Since then, she'd been prowling the house and drinking endless cups of tea.

She ran to open the door. Walker stepped inside. He looked tired. "Sit down," she said. "I'll make you something to eat or drink, or both..."

He grinned at her and took off his jacket. "Not just yet."

She stood looking up at him, longing to tell him what she'd said earlier that night when he hadn't heard her. But she could feel his exhaustion. He'd been through about as much as any man could handle for one night.

With gentle fingers he cupped her face, leaning down slowly. When they kissed it was as if they were coming together for the first time without barriers between them. Perhaps it was just that, for the first time, Marty felt totally committed. She wanted to spend her life with this man. Without him, nothing else mattered.

Her hair slipped from the combs with which she had confined it before getting into the shower. It tumbled around her shoulders and Walker wound his fingers in it.

Their bodies swayed closer together as if drawn by magnetic force, and their hungry mouths couldn't seem to part. She felt the hard firmness of him, so familiar, yet somehow new each time he held her, and she trembled.

When he let her go, she whispered, "I'm so glad you're here. I know you're worn out."

"I couldn't rest anywhere else. Not tonight." His big hand stroked her hair as he drew her tightly to him. She felt protected and safe in his arms.

She leaned against him, and they were silent for a long moment, drinking in the feel of each other. Finally she asked, "Would you like a sandwich? There's chocolate cake, too."

"Cake's enough—and milk."

They sat at the kitchen table. She moved her chair close to his, and he held her hand with one hand while he ate with the other. It was as if he couldn't bear not touching her, even for a little while.

"You were right, all along, Marty," he said. "I was a stubborn, blind idiot not to have realized sooner that you knew what you were talking about."

"ESP isn't a concept most people can accept easily."

"But I knew you. That should have been enough for me to accept anything you told me without question. I'll never doubt you again, you can believe that."

She squeezed his hand. "In the beginning, you didn't know me. You reacted as most people would have. Anyway, it's over now. How is Julia?"

"I think she'll be all right. She gave a perfectly coherent statement, and then her parents took her home." He finished his cake and she cut him another piece. He smiled his thanks and said, "Surprisingly, Danvers was eager to talk to us, too. He freely confessed to killing Linda Niles. He seemed to vacillate between wanting to unburden himself and wanting to convince us that he did what anybody in his situation would have done. The man's a raving maniac."

"I know. Julia told me he thought she was his sister."

"Yeah, he talked a lot about Rita. You were right when you said his problems went back to his childhood. According to Danvers, his father deserted the family soon after Rita was born. Evidently the family often didn't know where their next meal was coming from, and his mother took out her anxiety and frustration on him. If he was telling the truth, she abused him for years, both physically and psychologically. For some reason, she left Rita alone."

"That's not too uncommon," Marty said sadly. "Some abusive parents mistreat all their children, but others single out one child to be the scapegoat. Perhaps Danvers's mother identified the son with the father. A man left her in a difficult situation, but there was her son—becoming a man before her eyes—to bear the brunt of her displaced hostility."

"He said Rita tried to shield him from their mother's rages. She hid him and lied for him when she could. When she died, his world collapsed. He left home the same day. From what I could gather, Rita died in a hospital and, since he didn't stay for the funeral, he never saw the corpse. Maybe that's why he couldn't admit that she was really dead."

"Maybe he saw dying as desertion, and he couldn't believe Rita would desert him."

He nodded. "It was more acceptable to believe that his mother had lied to him, perhaps spirited Rita away to hide her. It became an obsession to find Rita and prove himself right. He started looking for Rita. If she'd lived, she'd be twenty-one now, so he looked for her where there were so many young women—the college campus. Both Linda Niles and Julia Allman had brown hair and eyes, so they were likely candidates. Linda quickly disillusioned him. She wasn't as clever as Julia. She screamed every time he came near her and, since Rita would never have done that, he decided he'd made a mistake and killed her. Julia managed to be convincing enough that he kept her alive for more than a month. The past few days, though, he was more and more sure that she wasn't his sister. He'd have killed her tonight if we hadn't been there."

"I know. Julia told me. It was probably only a matter of time until he'd have killed her, anyway. Such deeply troubled psychotics tend to explode periodically. He would have gone on killing if he hadn't been caught."

"He'll never stand trial."

"Just so he's where he can't hurt anyone else. As for you, you need to forget Danvers until tomorrow."

He finished his milk and she went behind his chair to knead the tense muscles in his neck and shoulders. His head dropped forward, and he groaned with contentment. "That's good. Why does it make me feel good, just to be with you?"

"I don't know," she said, smiling.

He tipped his head back and looked up at her. "Yes, you do. You know I can't make it without you." He took her hand and pulled her down to sit on his lap. He buried his face in her neck and inhaled her fragrance and heaved a sigh.

"That's nice," she murmured, "since I feel the same way about you."

He lifted his head and looked deeply into her eyes. "I've been meaning to ask you about that."

"What?"

"How you feel about me."

"You know. I think you must have known for a long time."

"I've hoped." His voice suddenly sounded hoarse. "I have to hear you say the words, Marty."

Her heart skipped several beats, then pounded furiously. He was so strong and sure of himself. But he was vulnerable, too, and it was that part of him that she saw in his yearning eyes. How foolish to think she should let him rest before she told him. He needed to hear it now, and she was the only person in the world who had the power to give him what he needed.

Holding his eyes with hers, deep and sure with the new confidence that rose in her, she cupped his face with her hands. Her fingers stroked the hard line of his jaw, and she felt his arms tightening around her waist almost painfully.

"Walker," she whispered against his beseeching mouth, "I love you."

"Oh, Marty, sweetheart. Do you know I've wanted to hear you say that from the first moment I laid eyes on you?"

She nodded and felt her eyes grow moist. Lovingly she touched his cheek. "I loved you almost as soon as that, too. But I had to know you wanted every part of me before I told you."

"I wanted every part of you, honey. Even before I saw Danvers's kitchen tonight. You believe that, don't you?"

"Yes." She slid off his lap and reached her hand out for his. "Let's go to bed now. You look so tired."

He let her lead him to the bed and pulled her down to lie beside him. "Not nearly as tired as I'm going to be in a little while." She tilted her head back so that she could look into his face. In the light from the next room, she could see the joy radiating in his eyes. She heard him catch his breath as she pulled his head down for her kiss.

The familiar magic took over then, filling her and carrying her to new heights of rapture, when she had thought she had already been as high as it was humanly possible to go.

A long time later, Walker murmured against her hair, "I might as well move in here with you. I'm here most of the time, anyway."

She snuggled against him with a contented sigh. There was laughter in her reply, "I suppose we could cut expenses by living together. Let's see, we'd cut the utility bills in half. It would be more convenient for both of us, too. And—"

Walker growled and stopped her words with a long, hot demanding kiss. By the time he lifted his mouth from hers, she felt all dazed and floaty again. "I don't give a tinker's damn about money and convenience," he said half-angrily. "I want to marry you!"

She wound her arms around his neck and said sweetly, "Goodness, I thought you'd never ask."

There was a pause, and then his laugh exploded. "I've been carrying around an engagement ring for a week, afraid to tell you, afraid you'd say no." He kissed her quickly. "Don't move. I'll be right back. It's in my jacket."

He came back and switched on a lamp. She was sitting up in the bed, and he placed a little black box in her hand. Inside, a diamond solitaire glittered against the red velvet. She was confounded.

Still standing beside the bed, Walker removed the ring and slipped it on the third finger of her left hand. She looked at him with tears of happiness in her eyes. "Oh, Walker, it's perfect. I don't know what to say."

"Say yes. You can manage that, can't you?"

Laughing, she drew his head down to hers and kissed him again and again. "Oh, I can manage that, all right. Yes, yes, yes . . ."

He slid back into the bed and drew her soft body against his. "Don't stop."

"Yes, yes, yes . . ." She kissed him some more.

Then the kisses grew longer and deeper.

Outside the bungalow, the wind rose and howled and rattled windows. Vaguely, through the magic spell Walker was weaving, Marty was aware of the faint smell of dust. Another storm was coming.

She murmured contentedly because she was safe in Walker's arms, where the dust storm could not trouble her. Nothing could harm her now. Their love—hers and Walker's—was strong enough to withstand whatever came.

AMERICAN TRIBUTE

Where a man's dreams count for more than his parentage...

Look for these upcoming titles under the Special Edition American Tribute banner.

LOVE'S HAUNTING REFRAIN
Ada Steward #289—February 1986
For thirty years a deep dark secret kept them apart—King Stockton made his millions while his wife, Amelia, held everything together. Now could they tell their secret, could they admit their love?

THIS LONG WINTER PAST
Jeanne Stephens #295—March 1986
Detective Cody Wakefield checked out Assistant District Attorney Liann McDowell, but only in his leisure time. For it was the danger of Cody's job that caused Liann to shy away.

AM-TRIB-1

Silhouette Special Edition

AMERICAN TRIBUTE

AMERICAN TRIBUTE

RIGHT BEHIND THE RAIN
Elaine Camp #301—April 1986
The difficulty of coping with her brother's death brought reporter Raleigh Torrence to the office of Evan Younger, a police psychologist. He helped her to deal with her feelings and emotions, including love.

CHEROKEE FIRE
Gena Dalton #307—May 1986
It was Sabrina Dante's silver spoon that Cherokee cowboy Jarod Redfeather couldn't trust. The two lovers came from opposite worlds, but Jarod's Indian heritage taught them to overcome their differences.

NOBODY'S FOOL
Renee Roszel #313—June 1986
Everyone bet that Martin Dante and Cara Torrence would get together. But Martin wasn't putting any money down, and Cara was out to prove that she was nobody's fool.

MISTY MORNINGS, MAGIC NIGHTS
Ada Steward #319—July 1986
The last thing Carole Stockton wanted was to fall in love with another politician, especially Donnelly Wakefield. But under a blanket of secrecy, far from the campaign spotlights, their love became a powerful force.